I0557851

Thank You For Supporting Our Dreams

CHRISTOPHER
PATRICK
STEFFEN

This is a work of fiction. If this resembles any actual events, locales, or persons, living or dead; I entirely empathize.

Cover Design by Michael Steffen
www.mcsteffen.com

ISBN: 0985909102
ISBN-13: 978-0985909109

for the unsung.
but only if they are working fulltime jobs.
and don't make enough money.
and don't have enough time.

CONTENTS

ACKNOWLEDGMENTS

The list of people that have helped me put this book together is painstakingly long. Almost everyone I have spent time with in the last three years has contributed some effort to helping me complete this work. For all of their effort, I am eternally grateful. I only hope they all forgive me for any errors or deficiencies still present in the current form.

For this specific work I have to thank Nathan Fielding for editorial help. I want to thank Jessy Poole and everyone in the King's English Writer's Group who provided feedback for early drafts of these stories (Christian, Chris C., Chris T., Annette, Sandy, Deb, and Meg, thank you). Jasna, Dave, Doug, Emily, Bob, Justin, Jamila, Amelia, and Andrew for reading the stories and providing feedback. Michael for providing the art at a moment's notice and giving me a tiny spot in FM during the Oakland Art Murmur.

I have to thank my parents for supporting my hopeless dream of becoming a writer. I have to thank everyone who has watched my life explode and reassemble these last few years. For my new Bay Area community including: my Frog Hollow Family (Mark and Carmen, Jess, Ashley, Mike, Andrew R., John, Eva, Jeff, Tomas); my FM friends (Peter, Joe, and Ofra); Write Club SF (thanks to Casey and Steven); Brian and Steve for Tuesday nights. I will never truly be able to thank Bob Leavitt, Justin Burch, Jamila Roehrig, Mike Abu (Abouzelof), and Jessy Poole for being there for me when I was drowning in valium (for a lifetime of inspiration and saving me, I thank and love you all). To my old Overstock family (Derek, Amanda, Elizabeth, Rebecca,

Matt, Craig and Yuri, Emily R., Rory) thank you (especially Josh Johnstun for proving this is possible and Emily Harrison for all and more). For Jasna, Sanjin, Hasan, Sonja, Denis, and Spencer for showing me what family is. For Zach Sampinos and John Clukey for continued inspiration. For Dave Combs, Doug Grose and Erik Henriksen for being my friends longer than anyone (I am honored). I am inspired by David Hunt and Curtis Jensen. I think anyone who visits or lives in Salt Lake City should know what Mike Brown and Angela H. Brown are up to.

I want to thank Andrew Jepsen and Emily Vigor for being honorary siblings to me. I owe both of you more than I will ever be able to repay you. And most importantly to Michael Steffen, without whom this book would not have existed and who exemplifies everything I hope to become: the Artist. I can count at least ten more people that should be on this list. Please forgive me if you aren't here. No one is forgotten. I love you all.

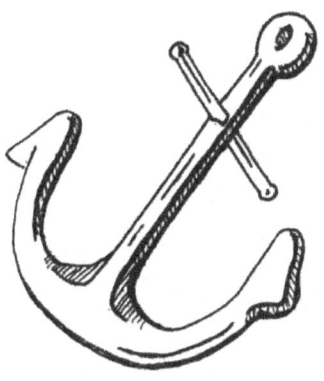

DEPORTING IN THE STORM

When the front door sticks Sean nearly shoulders it off of its hinges, the crash of which startles me and makes me worry he's going to break another one of our doors in half. This would be the third replaced front door for the House of Light in eighteen months. Bursting through the doorway, he looks at me on the couch and says, "I hate this fucking thing," jamming it closed, which causes a soft suction noise from the dimple-able lacquer of the painted front door and the misalignment of the door lock. He looks back at me one more time before quickly making his way to his bedroom. I can tell by the way he hardly makes eye contact and stalks away that one hundred percent of his focus is on what is probably a tightly bagged, somewhat stepped on 8-ball of coke he scored from the bartender of the restaurant he helped close.

I turn back to the boxy television procured from a pawn shop after Sean's flat screen "disappeared" and flip channels between a biography on Townes Van Zandt and a special about a town that was leveled by a tornado. In the footage of the town, the camera holds a tight shot of a wooden post with four forks stuck in the side of it. The foreground shot of the forks dissolves as the camera zooms out and the devastation of a church comes into clear view, most of the entire structure destroyed, but for a bell tower half-collapsed at an angle. The bell leans out of the tower; the wooden cross still clearly visible against the wooden tower's siding.

Sean's growing coke habit has begun to wear on me and the other housemates not so much out of our concern that he will accidentally white out his brain activity and flat line his heart rate while stark naked in his bedroom, but because the community that coke attracts. The House of Light is not prone to sleep, but there can be limits to the exhaustion one tolerates having to stay up past 3 A.M. on a Wednesday morning. E.g., I'm sitting on the metallic chair, the laser disco ball spins and draws multicolored, shimmering animal silhouettes across the walls, florescent fish dance in their immaculate 28-gallon aquarium, Derrick's turbo projector casts dancing images on the big screen opposite the fully-illuminated black-light posters, and more than anything I want the 43-year-old biker to stop giggling maniacally and to take his 19-year-old girlfriend off our couch and out the front door. I'm tired of playing babysitter to Sean's really weird friends when he disappears to buy beer for four hours.

On the television Townes wears a cowboy hat and holds a bottle of whiskey in one hand and a rifle in the other. Periodically he looks directly into the camera and says things, so I must assume he is being interviewed. I can't hear what he says, because the television is muted, and I have the record player playing some hot vinyl. It's a garage-y, lo-fi recording with overdriven vocals laid atop simple melodic harmonies that sound tinny and distorted. The music manages to sound contemporary and fifty years old. I bet my mom would have loved music like this when she was in her teens.

I have a thought and grab my acoustic guitar, which I

left leaning against the arm of the sofa. I strum a new little riff that I kind of like and keep playing it again and again. It's in E minor, which seems like every song lately but the notes are just so damn bluesy. Wonderfully so. The only words coming to mind for this growing melody are *Time again, baby…time again.* Won't be sure what this kernel will grow into until I really let the melody water the seed, but I keep playing and playing.

My phone rings so I put the guitar down and answer it. "How quickly can you grab your amp and guitar and be in the Aves?" Colin asks me.

"Um…what?"

"I'm at a party right now on J and 8th. Nantucket Nonesuch is going to start playing, but Mike D. said they are only playing, like, a 25 minute set. We could play after."

"It's, like, 11 P.M., right now. How am I supposed to—"

"You just be dressed. I'll get Dave to swing by and grab you. Dude, Allison is at this show. We totally got to play. I want her to see me rock out. She's never been to one of our shows."

"We haven't played one in, like, three months. Man, I feel pretty out of practice."

"We practiced last weekend. Dude. It. Is. Cool."

"That was three weeks ago. It's May."

"You need to see this party. I don't know where these girls are from. I don't recognize any of them. Be dressed. I'm going to call Dave. This is so on. We play tonight. Nantucket Nonesuch sees us again. They take us on tour this Summer. We split the van. Put out our CD with a real record label. Shows So. Cal. to Seattle. We blow this popsicle stick."

"Popsicle stick?" The line cuts.

I'll admit that two years ago when Mississippi Medusa first started practicing, I was excited. You carry the momentum of some inspiring band practices into a few energetic shows, where everyone in the audience roots for you, because you are new and cutting your teeth. You are different and brooding. And then you start putting all of the pieces together. You begin to think, yes, this is possible. I will be in a band that succeeds. We will never be an It band, because we're too ahead of the curve and too avant-garde for traditional radio play.... But we can fashion a loyal following. Maybe do the cult thing. Tour in a small van for years. Sell CDs through a respected independent label. Forge a life.

The first CD comes out and everyone in the band wants to wave it like a flag. Copies sell and you keep playing shows, but you don't make any money. And then time moves forward and the band practice keeps getting cancelled or rescheduled. You lose a drummer to an opium habit that turns into heroin. Your bass player starts to "love" his possessive girlfriend. The band retools and puts together some new songs. You still play shows, but you hate headlining. Everyone is quick to say hello, but nobody sticks around to hear you play.

The band is limping. I get that.

I love music. *Playing guitar is the only way you understand love.* April said that in tears, one of our last conversations. I don't think she meant for it to be an insult, but she had looked at me like I was a monster. We dated for four years, a large chunk of that time, while she was in college working on her Communications degree. She was probably the only person who never told me to go to school. I respect her for that. She had this soft red hair that used to swallow my fingers. Now when I think about her, I miss staring at her lips more than her eyes.

I thought I loved her. We loved each other. For years. People said we made a great couple. We would invite them to our apartment for homemade pizza. She and I were a team. She really knew how to decorate and turn our one bedroom apartment into a home. She made a great host, a grand coordinator. I knew my way around the kitchen. Learned to cook when I was ten. Given the time I preferred to grind my own spices.

When I moved out I took the records and my instruments. She kept the computer, the TV, our movies, the books, my KitchenAid, even my entire CD collection. For most of my moving out April stood still and watched me, entirely incredulous. Then she would start crying, and I couldn't say anything. Dave came in the apartment and helped move one box. He wouldn't leave the van after that. *I just need to keep an eye on the stuff, dude.* I don't blame him. The wreckage was all over April's face. I ripped out her heart and then walked away.

Writing music is the only thing I care about. I don't expect that to change. When you check the balance sheet, I have been in more bands than long-term relationships. That summarizes my life. These new songs are for a band of my own. Colin has Mississippi Medusa and some of my best riffs, but I want to keep these new songs under my control. They are something different.

I climb off the couch in the living room and head to my basement bedroom when I hear a yelp come from Sean's room. I stop in front of his door and knock.

"You ok, bro?"

"Just a minute." There is some internal shuffling: something is moved, a drawer is open and closed, the closet door slides either open or shut. Sean opens his door. "What up?" he says and walks over to his bed welcoming me inside. Every time I enter Sean's room a battalion of miniature armed soldiers confront in formation across the top of his dresser. There must be hundreds of these little Warhammer fantasy figures that at some point, Sean meticulously painted by hand with tiny paint sets and microscopic brushes. Each little figurine represents a tiny alien or robot soldier wearing a full suit of armor and holding either a spear, sword, or gun. The suits of armor have individual plates and panels with coordinated colorings that signify the soldiers' army. The attention to detail and decoration belies their light plastic construction.

Thousands of dollars' worth, he confessed to me one time over a four A.M. cigarette on the back patio, regarding the value of his collection of figurines. I knew he must be serious, because any time prior to that confession he would shrug and laugh as if to dismiss his collection as a pet interest. But that was just how he avoided attracting any real attention to it. This collection was his life savings, and I don't think he remembers confessing to me the value or he would probably be more paranoid.

"How was work?" I ask and drop onto his bed.

Sean wheels his wooden desk chair around underneath himself and sits on the edge of the seat leaning forward. He whistles manically and then says, "Man, dude, one of those evenings where I could just not..." he pauses and looks up to the ceiling above me while snapping his fingers, "could not, like, connect with any of the tables. I mean, I was there going through the motions, turning on the charm but it was as if every time I tried to...you know...really reach them, figure out what they were about, I would go right over their head. And they wouldn't really get what I was saying, and I couldn't clarify without complicating it? Know what I mean?"

Sean is speaking with his hands very rapidly and

weirdly his gesticulations don't match what he is saying. Rather than emphasizing what he is saying, it's as if his gesticulations are drumming out a separate counter melody.

"I think so," I say. "Like they just don't follow you?"

"Okay, okay. Like this," he says and the hands flail. I think this is free jazz speech. Some Cecil Taylor. Some very near death John Coltrane... "Someone asks for a diet Coke to drink, and I tell him that we only have natural organic sodas which I name but most are naturally sweetened, so maybe he would like some iced herbal tea? But the customer just looks at me blankly and says that a diet Coke would be fine.... I should have just said, we don't have Coke or Pepsi products, is what I should have said."

"Yeah, yeah, totally. Okay, I know what you're saying. What's up for tonight?"

Sean exhales and scratches the hair on the front of his head. "I'm thinking 80's dancing. I have some friends that are going. Sort of our Thursday night standard, right?"

"I hear you. Colin called me about a party in the Aves. Wants us to play a set at it. Sounds ridiculous so last minute...I mean shit, it's late. How will the cops not be called?"

"A party, huh? Could be cool. Could be cool."

My phone vibrates in my pocket, and I pull it out. My little brother is calling, so I nod to Sean and step out of his room while clicking the phone to life.

"Hey, Timmy, what's up?" I ask and walk down the basement hallway into my bedroom. I flip on the light, close the door, and drop onto my unmade bed.

"Eh...not much. Just sitting in the dorms...." My brother is in his first year of college, so I wish the glaze on the edge of his voice were from a few light beers, but know it is probably whiskey.

"What's up, man?" I try to hide the disappointment in my voice, to quickly cover my exasperated exhale. "How's school? This semester's pretty much over, right?"

"Yeah...sure. Classes are done. I've got one final left. Tomorrow, actually. And a paper to write. No big deal...." As I listen to him talk my eyes move to the CDs spread across my floor, piles of which have tipped to the side and slid over each other.

"You have a final...tomorrow? You sound a little lit. You gonna be alright?" I am really asking him about his scholarship. We have a background that qualifies for scholarships, but you still need to keep good grades.

"I'm fine, man. I have to be all moved by next Tuesday. 'S why I'm calling."

"You need help? Want me to help you move?"

"Not that. Is fine. Just to let you know I found a spot for the Summer. Mike and Jeff have an extra room...more like a closet, heh heh heh. But it works."

But for the grace of God. My brother and I aren't the praying type. Church was something that my mother tried to instill in us and that died with her. Right now, though, all I keep thinking about are those words. *But for the Grace of God.* But for God's Grace my brother and I didn't end up in a foster home. But for the grace of God I turned eighteen before my father was prosecuted the first time. But for the grace of God the public attorney ("Call me Phil...") helped me file the paperwork for Timothy's guardianship. But for the grace.... Saying grace: thankful to be working in a movie theatre full time to share one bedroom in the basement of someone else's house. Trying to chase Tim down when I'm not working: finish school, apply for college, apply for scholarships; meanwhile a manager is hassling me for not selling enough soda plus popcorn combinations.

Grace. I know what he wants to hear already…and I'm so tired.

Saying Grace. I used to think that praying for thanks before dinner was named after the children's mother. For us, Saying Grace. For Justin around the corner, it would be Saying Christy.

"It's upper Sugarhouse," Tim says. "Near the McDonald's. Just wanted to let you know where'd I'd be."

I mumble about that being good. Not far. There is a silence.

"Do you…do you think you could tell me about the pool?" he says. You never truly understand how exhausted you are until moments like these. This is when you feel like you are carrying the entire world.

"Sure, man." I reach for a good-natured, fatherly chuckle at this point, but my throat comes up dry. "We were just little kids, and we were at the pool—"

"I don't remember the pool. Describe the pool."

"Can't believe you never made it back out there. It's way out in Sandy I guess. Fine. The pool was kind of like every neighborhood pool: rectangular with the tiled lane lines along the bottom. In the shallow end of the pool there were some steps, and in the deep end there was a low-diving board. There was a patio area for grilling and picnics with a wooden cedar canopy that provided some shade above the tables. There were patio tables and chairs around the rest of the pool area, and you weren't allowed to run around the pool. On the side by the deep end, there was a large grassy area where people sometimes set up volleyball nets. You and I would just lie in the grass and watch the older kids do flips off the diving board. But mostly we weren't old enough to go off it."

"You could never do a front flip off the diving board."

"I know...I still can't. I don't know why. It's a weird mental thing. I'm still afraid of back-flopping." Tim laughs, and it's good that there is laughter. "So one time we were in the shallow end of the pool with mom. I think you were either on the edge of the pool or sitting on one of the steps, cause we couldn't stand, couldn't reach the bottom yet. Mom was teaching me how to do the backstroke, so she was holding me up while I showed her my strokes. I remember looking up into the sky and having to squint. Mom's face was all glowing around the edges from the sun, and I was looking right at her...."

That is one of my only memories of what you looked like, Grace. My mother the angel.

"Then we stop and suddenly look over, and you are gone. And Mom freaks out and starts calling out your name, and she's looking around the edge of the pool and over at our stuff at the table. I'm trying to look around under the water. Like maybe you sank somewhere, cause it has only been a few seconds, but the glare is really bright. Mom is about to climb out of the pool, when I spot you over on the other side of the pool hanging on to the edge looking at us with this big grin on your face. I yell to Mom and point to you, and she nearly melts down. She grabs me and drags me across the pool to you and is almost yelling at you, How did you get over here? What are you doing? You just looked at her and said, 'I swimmed.' You were so proud of yourself and Mom didn't even believe you at first until you showed us and did it again."

"I was only four."

"It was the width of the pool, but it was still a long way across. I bet you probably hadn't swum farther than eight feet before that and suddenly you were swimming, what? Fifteen or twenty yards?"

Tim laughs again. "How are you?" I ask him. "Are you ok?"

"How am I? Pshhh. I'm fine, bro. How are *you?* You are the one who has been in semi-meltdown mode."

"Meltdown mode?"

"That last month before you broke up with April and moved out. Man…. Calling me and asking the weirdest questions. You'd have a different 'Life Strategy' you called them, every time I talked to you. One minute you are moving to the City, then out to the desert, then up to Alaska."

"I had just realized that there were a lot of possibilities—"

"I think you said moving to Paris at one point? Really you just couldn't deal with the fact that you didn't love April anymore, because you fell in love with that one chick…Jessica?"

I never loved Jessica. We never could have lasted in a real relationship….

"But, I mean, it's ok, man. It's ok to fall out of love with somebody. You can't carry that guilt around forever. That's just the way life works out."

"Dude. In the scope of our lives, I'm not beating myself up about a break up."

"It was more than a break up. You guys were in love. You were a couple. It was the two of you for *several years.* But that's still ok. That's what happens."

"Thank you. Thank you, bro. I love the counseling from my drunken *little* brother. Seriously though—"

"How much weight have you lost?" he asks me. "Ten pounds? You look skinny. I bet you aren't eating regularly."

Technically, I had lost twenty pounds in the last four months. My skinny jeans had become baggy.

"I'm trying to eat vegan right now, so I'm mostly eating salads. It's healthier." Tim starts laughing again with a different type of laughter. I look at my guitar and amp. "I hate to bail on you, but you probably need to study and I need to get ready for a show. I'm playing a party in the Aves tonight."

"Good. You need to meet some ladies. Clean your dipstick."

I tell him to call me if he needs help with the move. I unplug my guitar and put it into its case and then climb behind my desk to unplug my amp and speaker. While on my hands and knees, I bump into the side of the desk which knocks my desk lamp over. It falls onto the carpet and the florescent light bulbs crack releasing this silty white powder. I can't remember, but I'm pretty sure that shit is toxic and someone stole our vacuum cleaner two weeks ago. I pick up the lamp and slam dunk it into my garbage can. Glass shatters with the crash. I collapse back onto my unmade bed. The fucking lamp is still plugged in to the power strip. Any moment Dave is going to call me from outside, and I'm still wearing my brown Carhart pants and flannel from work. My clothes have streaks of dirt from shipping grime and cardboard dust. Hello, ladies.

My phone vibrates, but when I look at it I don't recognize the phone number. On the line an automated voice tells me I am receiving a phone call from the county jail and assures me I will not be charged for the call. I have the option of permanently blocking any future phone calls from this location.

I accept the phone call.

"Paul? It's Dad. I need you to come get me outta here before they process me."

"How much is that going to cost? I have to call a taxi

right now?"

"Five fifty gets me out the door—"

"I don't have five hundred dollars. I don't even know if I have fifty dollars."

"Son, it's been a long evening...."

"Oh? Has it? What in the hell are you even doing there?"

There is a pause and then he says, "An asshole and I got into an argument about that new forward on the Jazz—"

"GOD DAMNIT...."

"Look...I understand this isn't what you want to hear right now."

"Yeah? You understand that? Well that's convenient."

"It would really be easier for me if you have the bail, but if you don't, you can call Bill at The Bond Brothers. He knows me and can come pick me up."

"I don't have the money."

"Fine. Fine...." he exhales loudly into the phone. "Call Bill. He'll take care of it."

He gives me the phone number, and I tell him it was nice to talk to him right before I hang up. There was a time when my father was an account manager. He wore a suit and worked in an office. His work clothes didn't include a name tag....

I'm still lying on the bed when Dave calls. Forget changing my clothes; forget the grime streaks and cardboard dust. I'll call Bill from the road and then work really hard trying to forget I still have a father. By the time Tyler gives us a count at the beginning of the set, all I will be thinking about is the time signature change after the first verse of Colin's new song.

THE SEDUCTIVE SHAPE OF SMOKE

The sirens wake me ten minutes before my alarm was set to buzz. I can tell that whatever is happening is very close, because I hear the sirens turn off and can still hear the truck engines growling in the cool Saturday morning air. It all happens on the far side of the house, but I make a point to look out my window anyway. Our backyard, with its wooden table cluttered with beer cans and bottles and unruly grass and weeds, looks neglected in a very un-Norman Rockwell sort of way. I turn my alarm clock off and step over the piles of wallets, bracelets, key chains, patches, and t-shirts I stayed up late preparing—the current cumulative assets of PorTown Designs.

I make my way to the kitchen where Nelly stands over the propane stove half-heartedly pushing around milky clumps of tofu scramble. She wears her thigh-high green thick-striped socks, and for a split second she readjusts her oversized pink terry cloth robe that she tries to bunch closed with her left hand. I steal a glimpse of a garter snap connecting to the top of her sock, and I shiver.

Seamus looks up from his copy of *Revitalize Your Business,* which is about as much of a Good Morning as I expect. I eye the coffee in his "Waterworld: Bad Movie, Worse Reality" mug and stumble across the kitchen linoleum catching my sock on the corner of a square of the laminate curling up from the floor. As I reach to grab a fresh mug from the cupboard above the sink, Missing Lynx, the orange cat scampers across the floor and begins purring as he pushes his head against my leg. I look down at M. Lynx, tickle the top of his neck below his ear, and then reach back up and take a glass tumbler, the last clean drinking vessel.

"Lynxie is hoping for wet food this morning," mumbles Nelly. Before her first morning smoke, Nelly runs on autopilot where even short sentences can challenge her.

"Lynxie is going to have to go out and get a mouse then, cause we got *nada,*" Seamus says. He uses the finger of his left hand to mark his place and holds his pencil above the notepad under his right hand.

Nelly's sleepy face curls into an accusatory scowl, her brow creasing above her large cerulean Pixie eyes. Seamus says, "Sorry, love, I've had no time. Let the cat out this morning, he'll be fine. We'll bring some food back this evening."

I pour myself a tumbler of coffee feeling like an invisible witness to these domestic spats. Though I pay a third of the rent for my room in the house, Seamus and Nelly know better than to expect me to feed their cat. I add a lot of milk and sugar to the tumbler trying to drown out the tangy discount flavor of the coffee beans. It's safe to say that the coffee maker could use a severe flushing of its lines.

For some reason I am remembering the night my mother threw my father out. My sister and I were playing Monopoly on the family room floor. I was about twelve, so my sister had to be nine. My father had just come home late from what turned out to be a bar, because he had been fired from the warehouse that afternoon. He had tried to overcompensate for his shame with rage by storming throughout the house, yelling about the bastard floor bosses and racial prejudices of black men giving jobs to black men. Monica was scared and for lack of knowing what to do, I told her to just keep playing and not worry about it. I had seen my dad drunk before, at barbecues at his friends' houses, or at the pizza parlor after my last little league game. In those instances the drunken belligerence rolled like waves between ebullience and fury, but the storm's median was always slightly more positive. This drunken anger was new, and I remember wanting to stay perfectly still while my father knocked things off the shelves, stormed into one room and out another, my mother in tow like a comet's tail. Monica and I both hoped he couldn't see us if we weren't moving.

Our stone expressions broke when he walked through the middle of our board game. With one heavy step in his boots, the cardboard sank into the carpet and then snapped, the hotels and houses went flying, an apt illustration of our world coming to pieces. Monica burst into tears pausing my father's tirade. My mother, unable to tolerate any more, screamed, "Get the fuck OUT!" I watched my father's expression shift as he stopped and looked down at us and then up at his wife. Seeing my mother's strength swung my father back from rage to a deep shame. He took one backward step off of our game board, looked down at the colorful bills I had fanned out in my hands and told me, "Never be at the mercy of another man; serve yourself." And then he walked out the front door. After that night, when we saw my father, it was as if he were an old friend of the family. A short time later he came to tell us he was moving to Los Angeles where some of his buddies said there would be work. My mother wouldn't leave our house on a whim and rather than pitch a fuss, he said he would call her as soon as he got some stable work and rented a house. I don't know if he ever called, but we never left Portland.

I walk over to the table careful not to step on M. Lynx, who makes it a point to dive his face into each of my feet as I step. "Did you guys hear those sirens? What was that about?"

Seamus pauses his reading with his finger and looks up at me. "You're on the other side of the house," he says and smiles, an obvious and almost bonehead statement that I want to counter by telling him and Nelly that I sleep closer to them than they think, which after telling them, I would wait a pause and then wink at them to convey, oh yeah, I can hear you at night. Seamus continues, "You missed out on the neighbors going into a full meltdown screaming match. I don't know how long it was going for, but it seemed like a while. Felony Flats."

"What in the hell is the matter with them?" I ask. Seamus shrugs as if there is an answer.

Nelly pulls the pan of eggs off of the burner. When she reaches up to the cupboard for two plates I watch how the robe climbs up the back of her stockinged leg from right above her knee to the middle of her thigh. "I swear I heard something…yelling about drugs, but I don't know if it was missing drugs, or wanting drugs, or stolen drugs…or just…drugs. I was sort of out of it until I noticed Seamus staring at me."

"I was waiting for a culminating gunshot," Seamus says. "Like a loud explosion that will definitively punctuate the screaming…I think I have watched too much television."

Nelly brings over the plates of eggs still clutching her

robe closed with her left hand, and Seamus sets his book and notepad aside.

"How's the business plan going?" I ask him. Seamus wants to put together a business plan so that he and Nelly can get a bank loan to open their own food cart in one of the downtown lots. For all of his studying, they haven't even decided on a type of food to serve.

"A lot to learn. It's harder than you'd think. I'm surprised some of the burnouts who have carts can pull it off." While never particularly motivated, Seamus can be intelligent and very analytical. Now whether a loan officer looking across his or her desk at the one hundred and thirty pound, six-foot-two string bean in mish-mashed, handmade clothes with size two ear gauges, greasy uneven hair, and tattooed arms will see a successful business prospect or a perverse wicked Santa elf who has made his way down from the North Pole, well....

Seamus and Nelly add some pepper to the puddles of yellow on their plates and then begin drowning the food in a vegan hot sauce. Not a bad strategy for fake eggs. Nelly looks at me sitting at the table in front of my tumbler of coffee and asks, "Do you want some of our eggs? We could get you a plate." Part of me could really use a little sustenance, but I still feel above taking the meager meals of skinny vegans.

"No, no," I say. "I don't want to eat this early, or I would. Thanks." I do begin cataloging the food in this house that I have bought: no more cereal, some dry pasta, three packages ramen, one softening apple. I should buy a box of oatmeal. I need some sales today.

"I just hope Verne isn't on one today. I don't know if I have the positive energy to combat one of her freak outs," Nelly says. Verne owns Bridge City Fudge and employs Nelly at the Saturday Market. Bridge City Fudge and my own PorTown Designs share a booth space, which means I am very familiar with Verne's freak outs. As we have moved further into Summer, I have discovered two things: my patience with Verne is inversely proportional to the thermostat and when we argue Verne will crack first. She may call me an asshole or a "capital-D dickweed," but she will be the one to grab her things and leave for the day in a fury of nagging. I like to believe that I can upset Verne, because she doesn't possess my spine and fortitude, but the fact is that I can't afford to leave the market early. I need every bloody sale I can hustle for PorTown, while Verne runs her booth as an excuse to eat carnival food and get away from her scrappy children for a few hours.

"You need to quit," says Seamus. He looks into Nelly's deep blue eyes for what seems like the first time this morning. "Spud's always saying he's going to drop Caleb. Kid hardly shows up half of the time. I can get him to take you on. We'd work together. It'd be perfect." Seamus works at a Did You Hear That elephant ears booth.

"Thanks, babe, but...." So many tacit arguments exist in the place she lets the sentence fall. She asks, "What would we do if that one stand closes?" Nelly kisses Seamus's cheek, a brief morning peck. What they'd do is simple: Nelly would take her clothes off to Eighties butt rock and Beastie Boys songs while tapping Lucite stilettos up and down a highly-polished stage. This is Portland.

On the plus side strippers eat better than we do.

The weather is so hot now that I will intentionally roll my thick dreadlocks under the showerhead, inflating my thick tubes of hair with water, because I know that for the couple of hours it will take my hair to dry my head will stay cooler. There is the unintended consequence of my hairline feeling greasy all day and the possibility that my hair will stink for a few hours, but I am willing to take that chance.

By seven A.M. I am stuffing the cumulative assets of PorTown Designs into my oversized messenger bag, along with my account ledger, a can of Coca-Cola, and one of my packages of ramen. A light hint of pot smoke wafts through my room, which cues me that Nelly and Seamus are almost ready to go. I fold the flap over my messenger bag, throw it over my shoulder, and cross the house to their bedroom. The door is open and Seamus crouches over a backpack packing his and Nelly's lunch. Nelly slouches back over the bed propped onto her elbows with her legs flopped over the side. She bats her heavy eyelids once in my direction while exhaling smoke slowly and tries to create smoke rings with the O of her mouth. The pot won't conform to the shape and dissipates. Her outfit would be unremarkable for her typical wear, vintage clothing snaked from The Bins, except for one noticeable difference: she is wearing a short denim skirt. Nelly almost never wears dresses or skirts. During the raging summer months, she will sport the occasional pair of shorts over a pair of leggings. Even now she wears a pair of eggplant tights, but I am still hung up on the skirt itself.

"Shall we go?" I ask.

On the bicycle ride across Southeast Portland, we slowly open our eyes to the waking morning, the sun rising to our backs and a light river fog burning away. It's going to be sunny today, which I hope brings people out, because I am low on cash and need to buy supplies. At KC's on 72nd, Seamus hangs a right to take us through the neighborhoods. We don't talk much on the way to the Market, our communication is more a series of changing bicycle order, a fluid leadership. Occasionally I am in front of us, and then I fold away and Seamus pedals ahead, leading us through intersections, until Nelly ends up in front of him and becomes our navigator. I watch her long legs pedaling; the denim skirt rides high. When I am directly behind her, the tight little curve of her ass makes me think of a teacup.

The route varies every time we ride with earlier rights here and later lefts there. We cross the soft hills like a school of fish, each sensing the change in route slightly before they happen. None of us are morning people, and at this hour are little more than the pedaling dead, but the slight breeze blowing against our face opens our eyes and flows into our lungs. I feel like my life is beginning and the possibilities are bristling just under the surface, and then we pedal under Burnside and I think of the row of homeless on the street above us, sprawled out in sleeping bags in a line in front of the shelter and I wonder how close I am to homeless. I have friends who have spent weeks under bridges, other friends who have had to live in cars.

We bundle our bikes together to a gate in view of the Did You Hear That booth, so Seamus can occasionally eye them. Because I have to set up my space, I leave Seamus and Nelly to chat for a bit. People arrive at the Market, erecting stands, and cooking the first meals. The smell of several grills heating up at one time, the grease breaking from gelatin to liquid, combines into a rich carnival-esque bouquet, appropriate for the sort of early morning shenanigans and joking that occur between the vendors. The crafts people lay out their inventory, cooks fire up their grills, and everyone cycles through the stands greeting each other and joking about how the week went, life outside the Market. A smattering of homeless wander amongst the booths attracted by the magnetism of collected human gravity, and the sporadic jogger passes, tracing the river-walk, but otherwise, everyone is united in shared entrepreneurial beliefs. At the most fundamental level we chase the American dream.

In stall 162, I set my messenger bag down and unfold myself a metal chair. Verne hasn't arrived yet, which more than pleases me, because I can work quickly to lay out the display of my goods. I am putting my t-shirts onto hangers when Kent, who owns the smoothie booth on the row behind ours, comes over for pre-game bullshitting. Only ten years older than me, Kent is an O.G. and my business mentor. I literally remember my mom taking Monica and me to the market when we were little kids and seeing a young scruffy Kent hang around with some friends and a mangy dog. Not long after I split the booth space with Verne, I went over to ask Kent about the business. Amused that I recognize him from so long ago, he fast became one of my favorite marketeers.

In his mid-thirties now, Kent traded in his stained, ripped jeans and tie dyed shirt for a pair of khaki shorts and rock climbing fleece. With the thick brown socks and fishing hat pulled over his shoulder-length straw hair, Kent made the conversion from scrubby teenager to yuppie, outdoorsy adult. Long lines in front of his smoothie booth tell he must be making decent money. His pretty wife and son always manage to visit in the later hours of the morning, she strolling around the front of his booth with one of her sharp hips kicked out and the little boy propped on it.

"PTown in the house," Kent says imitating a junior cheerleading squad.

"K. Smooth, how are you?" We slap side fives and pound fists.

"How is it, brother?"

"Oh…waking up this early on Saturdays sucks…." I say and smile. "I was at a party last night, just starting to talk to this girl, and I had to bail to go to bed. How in the hell did you ever meet your wife working a gig like this?"

"Easy. I stayed at the party talking to her, and then I rode the thick rails to work the next morning," Kent says tipping his hat up over a big grin, "if you catch my drift. But it sounds like you might avoid a thousand hours of community service and mandatory C.A."

"Yeah, but stay celibate….I'm sorry, I'm just kidding. I'm a whiny little bitch in the mornings."

Kent laughs. "Nature of the beast. Nature of the beast. Did you put together the budget I assigned you?" I turn to my messenger bag and begin rooting around it. Kent takes the mentorship seriously and assigns me little weekly projects. There is a part of me that would have laughed at the idea a few years ago; I did not waste my time with school. I think my opinion shifted when Kent explained to me how I could use my budget and why I would need it.

I hand the paper to him, and try to stand there with a stone face. Part of me is melting, because I spent several hours putting my budget together. It took me a long time to figure out some of the tricks on the spreadsheet program on Nelly's computer.

Kent scans the paper and slowly nods his head. I look around the market and see Seamus and Nelly standing in each other's arms. They are just past the line of the shadow from the Burnside Bridge and the sun turns Nelly's hair to gold. "I like this," says Kent, "but we don't know if it will work. The next step with your budget is to test it. We will need a few weeks for that."

"So my next assignment is to test the budget, see if I'm

good?"

"No, no. That's at least two weeks out, will maybe take a month. Next week, I have another spreadsheet for you to make. Do you have something to write with? Take these notes." I pull out a pen and Kent assigns me my most brutal spreadsheet, yet, full of formulas and calculations and sales percentages.

"And you have to count anything you give away," he says. In an almost caricatured fashion, Kent actually waves an instructional finger in front of me. "These analyses *only* work if you factor in *everything...*" Turning his head to the side, Kent sees Verne approaching our booth through the crowd toting her plastic cooler. "The more you fudge, the fatter your failure...."

"I got it, I got it," I say and start laughing.

Kent smiles. He hands my budget back to me as I finish up the last of my notes.

"Call me if you have any questions about how to get this junk to work. This isn't homework: it isn't worth you wasting your time trying to figure out how to do things. Just ask," he says. He turns his head back to his booth for a moment and then quickly glances up at the sky. It happens so quickly, I don't have a chance to tease him and ask if he really thinks he can tell time by staring at the sun. He distracts me by saying, "I have a friend who owns a boutique. I'm not going to tell you where, yet, but if you keep completing these assignments I'll introduce the two of you. It sounds to me like you are taking the business side of this seriously, and if that's the case, I'm not wasting my time teaching, and you won't waste my friend's time and flake out."

"I'm not going to waste anyone's time," I say.

"I don't think so, but actions speak louder than words. My friend has already had to deal with a bunch of flaky *artisans,"* Kent says the word like the idea sickens him. "They drop a bunch of their crap on my friend's store, disappear for months, and then come back, demanding money. I'm not tying my name to that shit."

Verne pulls her cooler around the back of our booth and Kent says hello to her. She grunts. I ignore her, because these wheels in my mind start spinning. If I can start selling my PorTown stuff every day, I can quit my day shifts at Better World Café. I could begin focusing on distribution. "That would be amazing, Kent. Tell your friend I'm really excited. I'm not going to let you guys down."

"If it can work, maybe it will prove lucrative." Kent shrugs. He walks away to say a few more hellos.

For five minutes, my mind pops at a thousand miles a minute with the possibility of making my living by selling my own designs, serving myself. Working day and night on PorTown, like some illusory dream, a bourgeois fantasy of possibility. I glance over and see Seamus and Nelly kissing now, steadily, but probably with a nice amount of tongue. I look down at the wallets spread over my booth's table.

Five shifts a week at Better World Café barely cover my bills. If I pick up an extra shift or two, I can buy some extra shirts, some extra ink. And if I lose a little sleep, I will have the time to use these materials.

The pendulum swings back and the heavy weight I sometimes feel clouds my mind. Verne breaks the clouds by pushing my wallets over to my half of the booth. The collared men's shirt she wears half hangs from the waist of her generic jeans, and her hair is pulled back into a clumpy bun. I would wager that she has been awake for twenty minutes today.

"Hey, Verne, it's Ernest," I say, a joke I never tire of

repeating. Her cheeks tighten a little bit.

"Dues are coming up," Verne says. She flips the top of her cooler back and bends to remove her brownies. "Rate's jumped twenty bucks. I'm going to need your half." She steps to our table and begins arranging her wares.

"What's this twenty bucks, crap? Rent isn't due till the end of the month," I say.

"That's Tuesday. I'm paying it now," she says.

"I don't have it *now*. It's not cool, I've got to pay it early just cause you get a bug to." I wonder how I can come up with $140. With my money put in the new shirts and wallets, I might as well magic its existence. "Pay it tomorrow. You can give me two more days' sales."

Verne huffs and for the briefest instance I imagine this new T-shirt design. It's a bull dog with long hair pulled back into a bun and Verne's lumber jack body overstuffed into high-waisted jeans and a tucked flannel shirt. I should come up with a title: Baby needs a treat! Something like that. I want to sketch this immediately.

"Fine. I need the cash tomorrow." Verne says and turns, finished with the conversation with me. She continues to sort through her cooler, rooting for different flavored brownies. I hear her mumble something that sounds like "that girl" and when I look over I don't see them standing in the sunlight. I wonder where Nelly is.

Getting strangers to buy your shit requires a fine balance between eye-catching presentation, unassuming salesmanship, and strategic bullying. Nobody slows his or her stroll without a gimmick. I am lucky: on the other half of my booth there is a paper plate with tooth-picked mini fudge samples. This does some of the hard work for me. In order to get people to stick around for more than five seconds, every weekend I construct a display out of PorTown items. To complete my illusions I add strategic LEGO people. This week it is a LEGO man floating away from his T-shirt desert island on a wallet raft with toothpick and patch sail. It doesn't take me long to set up my display, because I have already practiced putting it together at home, twice. I know it works, because often I see the same families with small children stroll over to see my creations. This group isn't my target audience, but they do provide sufficient crowding to draw attention to my stand.

I have attached bottle openers to almost every product I sell. I want PorTown's merchandise to be both distinct and utilitarian. I have uniquely designed art-nouveau type key chains with bottle-opening edges (cut by a metal worker friend of mine); I have also sewn bottle openers onto the side of T-shirts or stitched them into my wallets as well. It amazes me how many more shirts and wallets I sell based on these fifty-cent openers.

By ten A.M. the sun is blazing, the buskers are banging away on upside-down paint buckets and out-of-tune banjos, and the crowd is underwhelming in relation to the very decent weather. After bitching about the lack of sales, Verne wanders off leaving Nelly and me in peace.

"Where in the hell is everybody?" I ask Nelly.

She looks up from a notepad she doodles on and says, "No offense, but I couldn't care less. I don't think I'm feeling 'people' today."

I humor her with a chuckle and say, "Yeah, I get that, but my booth dues are coming up and I need to sell some stuff pronto." A family slowly strolling past a basket booth to my right looks over my desert island display. They stop to take fudge samples and look almost longingly toward Nelly, as if to suggest "This sure is some great fudge. Where can one find more fudge like this for later?" But Nelly has strategically turned and crouches over the supply bags, so that she doesn't have to make eye contact or talk to them.

After an uncomfortable minute of the husband and wife verbally complimenting the fudge, they look from the crouching Nelly to me. I say, "Handmade trinkets, jewelry, wallets, and bracelets. Great souvenirs and conversation pieces." They stare at me blankly and then walk away.

The moment they are out of earshot I turn to Nelly and say, "Geez, those guys were practically begging to buy shit."

She stands back up and smiles. "They could have asked," her eyes afire in her mischief.

I sigh, defeated in watching her cavalierly avoid the sales I desperately need. Nelly stands close to me, pokes me in the arm, and then walks her fingers all the way up my shoulder to ruffle my dreads. My heart drops, because this is the kind of crazy move that could tear our relative domestic stability in two. If Seamus were to see us, he would lose his mind and that would be that. I can't afford to go apartment hunting.

I step away from her. "Are you insane?" I whisper.

The smile Nelly throws at me sends a Mohawk of red flags prickling up my spine. She steps close to me and says, "I saw you checking me out this morning, when my robe parted. It made me bite my lip. Why do you think I did it?"

Some major dam up the Columbia River explodes and a torrential flood of water flows down the Willamette. The flood washes us away like the figurative matchsticks we embody. I'm thinking of last Wednesday when we drank too much, and I almost had to call in sick to Better

World Thursday morning. The night had been an almost legendary, drink-til-you-drop vinyl dance party. The turnout included a few people from Better World, some of Nelly's friends, and Seamus's friend Jeff. I don't think there was ever more than ten people at our home at a time, but the fervor with which we drank reminded me of being a teenager. I even threw up off the porch early in the evening and came back to drink more and keep dancing.

Everyone jumped around the living room, flapping and kicking out their favorite dance shuffles. There was a point when the music sounded especially smooth, like maybe we were hanging out in a swanky lounge in New York rather than a barren living room in Felony Flats. After one track finished, I collapsed on the couch. John, Seamus, Jeff, and Charlotte stepped out front to take a smoke break.

I tongued a piece of lime rind stuck in between my teeth from some tequila shots I took earlier. I realized I don't drink hard liquor very often anymore. In front of me Nelly flipped through the stack of records. I looked over her especially long back that was very visible through the forest green of her fitted t-shirt. She wore evergreen tree leggings underneath electric blue cuffed shorts with a giant black faux-leather belt in some Synthetic-Meets-the-Earth-Lover outfit. She pulled a record out of the pile, stood up, and put it on.

Vinyl ribbons of Portishead's *Dummy* flowed out of the speakers in sinuous waves that tickled the ends of my ears. I tried saying something about how this record is hypercool to Nelly who stood in the middle of the floor gyrating. She opened her eyes to look at me and took her hands out of her short platinum hair, like I had shaken her out of a daze. I brushed my dreads to the side and stared at her. A weighted dead space hung in the air between the gaze of two people staring at each other, alone in the living room in this small city in the middle of the week. We paused; I no longer heard the music and cast my line into the blue of her giant irises: I want you. She didn't say anything, but continued to hold my gaze.

Even as I said the words I wanted to reach out of my mouth and reel them back out of the air. But it was too late. Thankfully the front door swung open and people piled back into the living room, echoing accolades for Portishead. And we all began dancing again.

While dancing I stole a couple of glances at Nelly like a criminal who wants to watch the police investigate his crime scene. Maybe it was the haze of alcohol or secondhand pot smoke misting the living room air, but everything happened in heartbreaking slow motion. Nelly and Seamus, wrapped in a slow-tipping two-step in front of me, teetered to one side and then the other. Nelly's mouth pressed into Seamus's shirt, her head barely reaching over his shoulder, her face from nose up peaking over the wall like a naughty child, her giant blue eyes flapping their eyelash wings, fixing on me for a telling moment.

And I had to turn away and start twisting my head to throw the mop of dreads back and forth, clearing this air. Charlotte held one of her hands to her chest and stretched the other to the ceiling, while yelling, "Nobody loves me...it's true."

In the back of the stall 162 booth, Nelly continues to stare at me as if she can read my thoughts. This moment captivates me, because I feel the book in my mind flip a few pages forward. Then it flips back again to Wednesday night, but now the music was quieter out in the living room, and I had collapsed onto my bed without turning off the light or closing the door. On the precipice before unconsciousness, I sensed the light turn out in my room and I rolled in bed enough to see someone in the doorway. My vision pulled together on Nelly who slowly stepped across the bedroom, bent over my bed-ridden body, and slowly licked my cheek. My heart rate raced so high I thought I might Belushi-out, and the adrenaline threw me into a paralysis. I passed out and thought I had dreamt the whole thing.

Still reading my thoughts in the back of the booth Nelly stares me straight in the eyes, says, "I like the taste of your salt."

This moment, not the party a few nights before, but this exact second determines the next five years of my life. From this burning ember, the flame that consumes PorTown will flare, half of my possessions will be abandoned, a stable home in Southeast Portland will incinerate, and all of my current dreams will waft away in the smoke that clouds my eyes and makes it difficult for me to speak to Kent for a few years.

I will rise again from these ashes, an incarnation even more resilient and capable than now, a phoenix starting over with wings flared...a few years down the road.

In the meantime I roll in the fire of searing sex.

In the future I will joke: I fucked the vegan out of a girl. Five years of my life reduced to an eight-word quip.

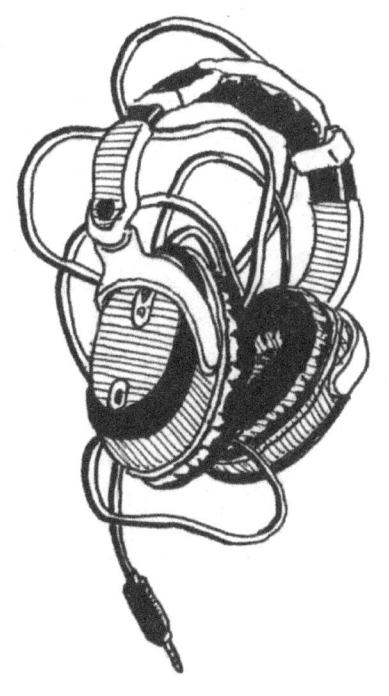

A STORY FOR LA MANO

When Jorge yells for me to leave the register and head to the back of the store to help unload the produce truck, I reach for my chain, kiss the crucifix and whisper *Dios mio*. I can stand to work the register, to deal with the old people trying to take discounts where there aren't any, or the homeless trying to trade bottles for money. I can stand gringos griping about the five dollar minimum for credit card purchases, or the way they hold their grocery carts up near their chests like they're constantly afraid of being pick-pocketed. I get a high from the energy of these people. Their rhythms—I absorb them into my blood, intermingling with my own heartbeat, creating this counter-rhythm, like a step's echo, pushing my ideas with syncopated swing up into my brain that I kick out into my lyrics. It's how I channel my art.

But there are mornings when the fog rolls in with a little too much bone-chill, the Chinese next door strip fresh duck carcasses, and the smell from the sidewalk urine makes a bad creep into the front of the store. I'm thinking: get me the fuck out of the front for five minutes, and like lightning pitched through the darkness by St. Miguel, the *veduras* boys buzz the backdoor. I'm saved. Amen.

Roberto and that Argentine, Emilio, have already begun stacking crates of tomatoes, cabbage and onions. I roll the dolly out the backdoor, and receive a *¿Que pasa, chico?* and a slight smile from Emilio who is clearly amused by the joke he has made by using the wrong gender. I say in English, "Nuthin', suckas."

I find I take fewer smoke breaks on the days approaching garbage day, on those last days each week when the air in the alley behind the mercado fills with a pungent funk from our rotting produce and meat, and the seafood and *solo dios sabe* from the Chinese's dumpster. Not even cigarette smoke can combat the waste syrup that seems to condense right from the air in one's nostrils, cause simultaneous sweat and stickiness on the skin, and the eyes to blink and itch. On those days the flies swarm in full frenzy like a tickling cloud, and there is the constant rustling from the heaving mercurial tide of rats ripping through the plastic bags. Unloading trucks becomes an exercise in constant movement and breath control. I move so quickly that I have to reward myself with a bonus two minutes in the walk-in, slowing my panting to a steady breath and feeling my pores close and squeeze out the stink's poison.

Because the garbage truck rolled through yesterday, the alley is a rather shady respite and I remind myself to grab my roll of bidies from my parka pocket so I can suck up a bonus minute of this solitude. I scan the alley back to front for any bums trying to catch pause away from the street or junkies thinking they've discovered a temporary shooting gallery. Satisfied it's clear, I look at a new graffito of a rat skull and some call letters. Probably a shorty learning how to use a can, no flourishes from fat or thin caps, but your basic Krylon ripped right from a drugstore's shelf. I'll try and talk Jorge into letting me take a half hour this afternoon to cover it.

I slide the dolly under a stack of crates, tip everything onto the wheels, and drag it back into the store to the empty spot in front of the walk-in refrigerator. In the back of the store, Carmela, Jorge's wife, sits at the desk punching numbers into her adding machine and reading over papers. All day long, little Carmela sits at the desk, her stubby squat legs crossed at the ankles and tucked under her chair. Her purple-framed reading glasses with matching neck strap perch on the edge of her nose, and she always coordinates her outfits with sparkly costume jewelry. For as much of a *cabron* as Jorge pretends to be, Carmela is the backbone of the Esperanto Mercado. She balances the store's books, runs the payroll, maintains business licenses, organizes the inventory and even places the orders. Without her the store would close in a week. Jorge can't add or subtract his way out of paper bag, yet he stalks through the store with the machismo of someone who handles everything. He is dumb as a *burro,* and it drives me crazy to watch him take her credit.

Every morning Carmela and I share a routine where I show up at work in starched baggy jeans and a jersey or some oversized shirt with my hair tied in a long single braid that falls from my Giants hat. Pequeña Carmela stands up from her desk and shakes her head with mock disapproval, while she walks over to me. She pinches the shoulders of my shirt to straighten it, while saying, "*Mi pachita hermosa,* why must you dress like a boy? Such a pretty girl. How will you find a husband?" I haven't the heart to explain some things to her. She is my *Otro Madre* or even my *Buena Madre.* If my real mother were to try to do the same thing to me, I would be tempted to slap her. Instead I reply to Carmela, "I am happy." We stand there for a minute, and she lightly brushes my cheek with the top of her hand.

Stacking the crates near the walk-in fridge, I turn and head back out to the alley. In the back of the truck Emilio carries and drags crates to the edge for Roberto to pick up and set in stacks for me. I drag another dolly load inside and when I return they both sit on the back of the truck with their legs dangling.

"When are you battling next, Aliento? Emilio doesn't believe that girls can make great rappers," Roberto says in Spanish.

"They cannot rap in the true Tupac, hip hop sense." Emilio shakes his head and waves his hand. "A girl can say a rhyme, but it takes the lion heart of a man to express true art."

In English I say, "The lion heart to express true art."

"See? Genius," says Roberto.

"You rap in English or Castellano?" Emilio asks me in English.

"In English. Any *puta* can rhyme words in Spanish." I watch the wheels turning in Emilio's head, but can see where his thoughts mash up against his thick skull.

"I am making an album. Tonight I can put a few songs from it onto a CD and give it to you guys on Monday."

"Bueno!" says Roberto. He pops from his seat off the back of the truck and hands me the invoice to sign.

Behind the register I keep a sheet of notepaper to scribble thoughts one bar at a time. I have to build every verse brick by brick. Whenever I begin to create some momentum a customer comes to the register, interrupting my internal rhythm, leaving me to restart the engines. This happens ceaselessly.

Felt and Tasha walk in the front of the market. Felt says, "Sup, Breath?" and greets me with a sliding five and knuckles.

Tasha says, "Hi, Ali," and then makes her way into the market. I watch her step away from the counter, eyeing the sway of her hips.

Felt catches me staring and smiles. He leans onto the counter and says, "You gotta get to a dyke club. Your mind's gonna go loopy."

I agree with him, but say, "A femme ain't a straight girl. Besides I barely got time to eat once I finish with this place." I think of the round melons Shannon's ass used to make in her short skirt. She knew how to walk away from me, pivot on a heel, and disappear into the dark with a flock of her little girlfriends in a wake behind her.

"No doubt," he says which frustrates me a little bit. Felt makes change dealing nickels and dimes of weed and gets to live with Tasha rent free, while she goes to Golden Gate University. Her parents, living back in Boston or Connecticut, pay all the bills and rarely visit. Twice yearly, Felt throws on his only striped sweater and skinniest pair of jeans, and shakes Mr. Tasha's hand, saying things like, "Yes, sir. Of course, sir." Two days a year of playacting and as long as he doesn't get caught in some other girl, he can mope around the rest of the year. The envy can grate on me.

I dream of an alternate life where I don't have to stand in the doorway of Esperanto fifty hours a week, where my eyes don't burn every morning, dry from lack of sleep; and I don't have to wake up before the apartment is warm, buried under thick blankets and tip toe around so many sleeping bodies. I need a little space of my own.

"You comin' by after?" he asks. On the plus side, Felt and Tasha take me in like family, and I spend as much of my free time at their place as I can. I think my proximity to Tash is seeding the crush. I look into her eyes after I have been at work all day and my mind blanks. I notice things around the apartment like the new towels in the bathroom, the new prints hanging on the wall above the kitchen table, or that a large pile of dishes that Felt left in the sink is now washed. I appreciate the way she takes pride in their home, and it inflates my heart. All of that energy, I channel into my music. I should have disclaimers on all of my recent love songs saying, "For Tasha."

"Of course. We need to finish this damn song." On Tuesday, Felt finished a beat that used one of the craziest horn samples I have ever heard, something he found buried deep in some hard bop B-sides. We started freestyling around the mythological idea of a Street Knight, listing his attributes and accolades. The concept stuck and so we started writing the chorus and verses for the song. With three solid hours, I might have finished the song in one sitting, but I had to dam the torrent of free-flowing rhymes and drag myself home to get sleep for work. For the last couple of days and nights, I have been writing rhymes while at work and recording sections at night. Every morning I start throwing coal on the fire with hand-scribbled rhyme notes so that I can have the engines up and gunning at night when I step behind the microphone.

Street Knight follows the exploits of a hero set in L.A. during the zoot suit riots and Depression era, running around the ghettos at night, protecting the day laborers and leaving a little money and food for the poor. His real name is Manuel Flores, but everyone calls him La Mano, because he attacks slum lords and corrupt police without using guns. The Latin ghettos need these heroes. I want to re-create a mythology that was lost when the Europeans smashed Latin icons and burned our books.

People are lost without a collective conscious. I want to create a concept CD called Buried Heroes, where every song is about a different heroic figure that has been lost in history or deliberately repressed.

Tasha comes to the counter holding the basket of assorted groceries in front of her with both hands. The way she holds the basket creates a deep V of her arms that evokes a million images of graceful actresses and smooth-skinned models. Some women have a way of moving that mesmerizes me, I feel punched in the back of the head every time I see it. How can someone do something as simple as holding a basket of groceries well? Everything about Tasha's look makes me want to squeeze her into a giant bear hug. She wears a white puffy down coat with faux fur lining around the hood, matching white sweat pants that have been pulled up with the waistline rolled over, and yellow flip flops. Her hair is still up in a bun, her entire look suggesting that she rolled out of bed moments before coming to the store. Breathtaking.

"Hey, sugar," I say, which causes her to blush coyly and makes me feel like my attentive eye has been rewarded. There is a sparkle in her smile from the tongue stud. I take the cart and punch severely discounted prices into the cash register, at least fifty percent off. I don't take discounts for anyone else, but Felt and Tasha are an important part of my family. They never buy much either. As much as I am over at their place, Tasha might as well be buying these groceries for me.

They pay and leave and a homeless man asks to buy five cigarettes using his nickels and dimes.

Coming out of Esperanto I walk down Capp toward Market as the amplitude of rush hour noise frequency softens into its early evening lull. I turn west onto 16th and the sun is low enough in the sky to bathe everything in bright colors that I have to mute with my sunglasses. Washed in gold, the crowded sidewalk jams tight with taco vendors, *pequeñas madres* and their trail of *pachititos,* souvenir shops spilling onto the sidewalk with Ave Maria candles, T-shirts, and posters. The homeless stay against the buildings waiting for gringo tourists so they can make their play. I drink the sunlight through the skin on my face, which feels like recharging internal batteries. Until Sunday afternoon, I spend most every day in the shadows or under artificial light. With direct sunlight in my eyes it's hard to see the tags scribbled on the buildings or garbage cans, loose trash piling in the gutter or against building nooks, or even the dirt worn into the pants and shirts of the panhandlers. I want to accuse the sun of dishonesty for its gold washing, and the thought makes me sad.

The cool evening air is laced with hints of a brisk ocean breeze that pierces my skin. Though I can't see it, I know that fog is on its way and maybe even rain. I wonder if this is a sense that only coastal people have. Like, how can you tell rain is coming in the Midwest? Maybe you can see the clouds; maybe you smell it. In San Francisco, you feel it.

Eventually I reach Duboce where Tasha's apartment window makes the left eye of the face of their three-story building. Their front light isn't on, which causes the building to wink at me. I take this to mean either that Fate is on my side this evening and Felt and I will lay down the rest of that track, or the universe is about to prank my opportunities again and I shouldn't take life so seriously, because it always has the final laugh. I buzz my way through their front door and take the three flights of soft carpeted stairs.

Tasha opens their door and I step through the

doorway before kicking off my shoes. Without her puffy coat and in a pair of reading glasses, Tasha looks domestic, the way you see a mug of hot chocolate. She has shed several shells from when she was at Esperanto earlier. Even though I already know, I ask her what she is doing. She tells me that she is reading for one of her classes.

"Anthropology of Early American Civilizations. Mostly it's how Native American and early Latin American societies worked. There is soup simmering on the stove that should be ready in a little bit," she says. She walks over to the stove and stirs the soup with a wooden spoon. She raises a spoonful to her lips and blows it cool before taking a sip. Then stirs the soup again and adds pepper. I think about Shannon's lips tracing a line down from my ear to shoulder. It's the closest I came to letting her fuck me.

"If you keep feeding me, I'll never go home," I say. The moment I say it, I begin wondering if I am overstaying my welcome. I don't know why I said anything other than thank you. I'm disarmed by insecurity and can't figure out what makes me talkative this way. In my life, how is this the only time I feel nervous? I flash a weak smile that insecurity tightens at the edges. Tasha smiles warmly and then walks back to the couch to her book.

A little of me stays with her in the front room, but the rest walks into the bedroom where Felt sits cross-legged on the floor playing video games in front of their small television. With his hat turned crooked backwards and his mouth hanging open, he looks more like a fourteen year-old skateboarder than my dynamic twenty-four year-old partner in rhyme.

"What up, Breath?" he asks. His tongue, sticking out

of the corner of his mouth, darts back and forth as he concentrates on his game play.

"Another day in paradise. You want to finish the song?"

"Yeah, yeah, yeah," he says. "I'll pause this." I walk over and sit at one of the two chairs in front the desk that holds the turntable and sampler. For a full two more minutes Felt keeps playing the game, and I start wondering if tonight is going to be a total waste. How long do I have here before I need to head home? I feel a hot envelope plump with cash burning a hole in the inside pocket of my coat. It feels like a drama magnet. I start cursing myself for lazy collaborators. My synapses flash a mile a minute, and I envision breaking Felt's neck, licking Tasha's tongue stud, and exploding through the front window.

Felt finally pauses the game and comes over to the desk. My mind pops too quickly and I am in the wrong mood to try and write my last verse for Street Knight. The words pouring into my mind are all attack-barbed and prickly with venom and acid, street battle rhymes with punchy breaks, ready to knuckle up on a motherfucker and disassemble him. Loud drum beats and high hat crashes, the drum rolls of a battle advance.

I try to get a hold of myself, whispering Hail Mary's to myself in English, an almost painfully unmelodic prayer; its a-rhythm calms the raucous beats in my head. Oblivious to my meltdown, Felt rolls a skinny joint on his dresser and lights it taking a few sucking hits to cherry the end. He knows not to bother offering me weed and walks over to the desk and begins turning everything on. He plays the Street Knight beat so I can finish writing and practice my last verse. I ease the Hail Mary's and start listening to the looping horn blowing its brass mind to pieces and the syncopated drum crashes.

Every time I listen to one of Felt's beats I begin to think of all of the potential locked away in his lazy mind. Without a quality sound board or a decent Roland, Felt is a zero-budget maestro who can make beats that rival some of the best producers in the business. Part of me worries that my rhymes will be lost in this orchestra. I take the folded notes out of my pocket and start reading my most recent scribblings. *And the culminating downfall / rose drops its final petal in a test of mettle....*

Street Knight will actually have two endings in this final verse. The first ending represents the hero myth where La Mano is killed in a hail of gunfire after the police spring a trap for him and a cousin rats him out. This will be the hero ending, but the verse will quickly dismiss this ending as a fantasy and construct the real ending around the idea that Manuel Flores's warehouse will close, and he will have to struggle so hard to make money, he won't have the time or resources to continue the La Mano tradition. He will work three jobs paying his mother's hospital bills and then he will die a few years later himself. It's real, inglorious.

Outlining it for Felt takes effort. "Why strip his myth after we spend the whole song creating it? I mean, we're creating a legend and then you just make it a street song."

"That's the point," I say. "*Niggas ain't sippin' wine / niggas sippin' apple boon / this ain't no white cartoon.* Hip hop's not a place for fake fantasies. The myth becomes more real if we set it in a realistic setting. There's no hero that gets blasted in gunfire. There's no heroes."

"It seems like a copout to me," Felt says. He tokes the joint. "The song builds this level of momentum so that it can basically explode by the time we hit this final verse. I am layering extra drum rolls for this verse so that it is this mind-melt cataclysm and you want to turn it into some Tupac verse. I'd feel manipulated listening to that. I wouldn't think to try and look it up. I want kids going to the net over this shit."

"It's real life."

"What's real life, Breath? Momo getting took in Chinatown is real life. Jamie getting stabbed in the TL walking through at the wrong moment. The Emeryville show with the gunfire we had to run from. Now what? You want to take a street legend and have him die like ninety-nine percent of the city. Who gives a shit? If anything, we should say that the rumor was that the police tried to say that they got him, but there was no body. We should keep the image alive. The legend should stay fresh. Like Zorro."

"You slipped, *loco*. Nobody's trying to reissue the Zorro myth," I say laughing. Felt starts laughing, too, like he realizes what he just said. "That dude is soil. A cartoon. I don't want that, but I don't want Batman either. The police aren't the bad guys. We could write a G song for that. The system is what's unbeatable. The system is designed to feed off all of us."

"Go back to the Haight, you fuckin' hippie," says Felt.

I laugh. He's still skeptical of the idea so I rap the entire verse. I make the ending dramatic, pour my heart over it. This isn't some hollow whimper song; this song rages. The last few bars go from a shout to a scream. Felt says, damn, let's get that. He sets the mic up in the walk-in closet and hands me the headphones. He hangs the blankets we use for damping external sounds. Our sound booth is less than ideal. We record vocals in his and Tasha's walk-in closet to drown out the city noise. It's a pretty raw experience because there's not even a light bulb. You put the headphones over your ears in the dark

and it's like the universe consists entirely of the song.
There are times where a Felt beat can drown you
completely in its layers and you don't even realize you are
mumbling your words. My problem is staying focused.
I've always got to stay focused.

While Felt tweaks knobs and sound checks the mic, I
try and blank my mind so that I'm not trying to repeat a
half-hearted copy of the verse in the way I just performed
it. It's better if I get in the booth with my mind clear and
just rip it from scratch. My heart's pounding heavy and
suddenly I'm thinking about Shannon, remembering her
soft body pressed against me with the window open
during the summer. I used to trace my fingers over her
breasts and recite rhymes to her when we lay in bed after
sex. She used to say that she couldn't fall asleep without
hearing the sound of my voice. Eventually she was spun
tight enough, she didn't even try. She weighed less than
one hundred pounds, a bouncing sprite I could
occasionally lure into bed for fifteen or twenty minutes
before her mind would wander, and she would be back in
the front room swallowing pills with her roommates,
talking about television.

It ended ugly. Weeks of dramatic screaming matches,
her eyes aflame, giant pupils threatening to swallow
everything like two black holes. Her hair had grown
stringy and her skin was becoming sallow, but I couldn't
say anything without hearing a tirade about the girls she
had to deal with at the salon or some drama with one of
her roommates. All of this negative energy would become
my fault, or I would have to deal with the repercussions.
More than once, I had enough and walked out the front
door of her house, her screaming that I'm a shitty fuck
from the doorway, me having to hoof back across the
Mission at three A.M. for a couple hours of sleep.

The final blow up was in a dirt pit rock bar called Chronos surrounded by every butch, dyke, and femme we knew. Shannon wore an eight-inch vinyl mini skirt the color of key lime and a black mesh top with a very visible bra beneath it. In her four-inch heels she was almost as tall as me, so that I could look her eye to eye. She must have spent hours getting her hair to curl and hang in those tresses.

We only went to Chronos when someone came into town that made tolerating the moldy smell and ripped bar seats worthwhile. It was the type of bar that didn't own any martini glasses and the tables and counters were always dusty with cigarette ash even though no one was allowed to smoke. Most Chronos nights had ended with Shannon and me stepping back into the Bay air smelling of stale cigarettes, acrid sweat, and spilled alcohol. If I were lucky, I could sleep in the next day; if I were crazy, I could nap for three hours before work.

On the last night I saw her, Chronos was packed tighter than I had ever seen it. On top of the usual Friday night crowd, a popular gay DJ had come from LA to spin records bringing out the entire LGBT crowd and half the hipsters in the city. It took us twenty minutes to fight our way in the door, and almost immediately Shannon abandoned me in the drink line. I bought us beers and wound my way through the crowd running into Dana standing near the bathrooms. He smiled at me, making two air kiss salutations, and asked me how I liked the music.

"Shannon and I just got here like ten minutes ago. Have you seen her?"

"She and the other pixies fluttered their way into the bathroom a few minutes ago...I guess they haven't finished up yet."

I know he could read the drama on my face, because his mouth curled with slight disgust. He shrugged and walked away from the wall he had been leaning against.

I found them in the last stall snorting bumps off of Shannon's unfolded compact.

"You fucking told me, you weren't going to do that shit tonight."

Shannon snapped the compact shut and threw a blasé, annoyed look at me with her oil-slick pupils, shining even more brilliantly in contrast to her ever-worsening pallor. Michelle and Julie went paranoid quiet and froze as if to hope that they wouldn't be noticed. Their hands twitched in little automatic gestures making adjustments to their outfits, their effort to appear natural, though their eyes never left me.

"What do you want me to say?" Shannon asked and shrugged the thought off.

"I got your beer," I said raising the stein. I always thought the large plastic steins at Chronos made a funny visual contrast in the hands of a tiny, dolled up femme. She took the mug from me and said thanks, pivoting on her heel.

Before she could walk out the bathroom I grabbed her hand, turning her toward me. A small splash of beer from her mug leapt from the stein and fell to the floor. The oil in Shannon's eyes went aflame. I shrugged and said, "What? Is that it? You PROMISE to stay clean tonight and two minutes after being here I catch you in the bathroom."

"What do you want?" She lifted her arms to shrug and more beer spilled from her stein. When it splashed on the ground she laughed. I wanted to tell her that I wanted the girl I loved back. I wanted the girl that smelled like lavender when I woke up on Sunday mornings. I wanted my Saturday-morning-cartoon companion in little cotton pajamas with the tiny daisies.

But I was going to call her a fucking junky, when she beat me to the punch. Still smiling over her stein, she waved her arm toward me and said, "Have some." In the slow motion rise the arc of beer made from its glass I recall a split moment where the briefest flicker of light sparkled across the flying liquid before it descended onto my shirt.

I don't remember where my beer stein went, but I know it wasn't in my hand when my punch destroyed the paper towel dispenser. Leaving the bathroom was a haze, but Shannon followed me back out and across the entire club screaming after me, our friends already formulating their own versions of the story before the scene had ended.

I hadn't been out to clubs since then. Working long hours and working on the music. Focusing on anything to change this situation.

"Breath!"

It's not the first time Felt has said my name into the headphones. I reply and he says he is going to queue the track. He asks me if I am ready.

Street Knight starts playing into the speakers and takes me back to the story of La Mano. For a moment I feel like I can see L.A. from the golden years of Hollywood. Then my pocket begins vibrating and interference stutters over the microphone lines.

"*Ya, ven a casa.*"

I step out the closet and Felt says, "Dude, was that your cell phone? You should have left that out here."

"My mama texted me. I have to go."

"Shit, Breath. When are we going to finish this…" but

he isn't really asking. He knows that I can't stay. The cash in my pocket is on fire. My mom sits at home, probably waiting for some money to go buy groceries. She needs me to watch the little ones.

The air will be nice tonight. I will practice the verse again on the walk home, and maybe we will finish the song tomorrow.

REBUILDING THE LEVEES

One afternoon I met Tony in the rotating Carousel Bar in the Monteleone Hotel. We drank Cuba Libres and made small talk with the bartender, a friend of Tony's. Not working tonight, I usually found Tony behind the bar of a small place called The Copper Plate on Bienville that attracted me with the rock n' roll ambience I missed from the bars back home. The Copper Plate lacked the fancy cocktails of Bourbon St. or a row of televisions blasting sports wrap-ups. Through the dark lighting one could make out a few tattered concert posters for Led Zeppelin and The Clash poorly taped to the wall. I got to know all of the bartenders at The Plate, but in particular, Tony, who was only a few years younger than me (he was twenty-two), became a fast acquaintance and would often lead me around different Quarter haunts. Tony had been at The Plate for two years and worked at Lafitte's (the blacksmith bar) for a year before that (don't ask how). He was the one who introduced me to much of the working crowd I was to meet during my stay. He also championed my writing, and while I couldn't get any pieces into the *New Orleans Weekly*, I was able to get a few things into little French Quarter zines.

Back in the slowly-rotating Carousel Bar, Tony's

bartender friend, Charlie, kept pace with our rotation (the interior of the bar, where the bartenders worked, did not rotate) and told us about a bar-hopping party that was being thrown for another friend of theirs, a server from the famous oyster restaurant around the corner.

"I don't know how thrilled I am to go roving the gay bars with a bunch of queers while Deon tries to score curious farm boys and discreet business men," said Tony and then turned to me. "Deon's straight as a fish hook."

"Suit yourself," said Charlie while shrugging, "but the only good pussy out tonight will be singing Happy Birthday for Deon's twenty-fifth. You know that boy only has two types of friends: queers and delicious women."

"I'd be willing to gamble on that," I said.

A lot of noise came from the hotel lobby with the arrival of a convention group. After a lull in the lobby noise, the bar filled up with graphic designers from some major internet company. Tony and I took a couple of bar rotations chatting to heavy-set women from Iowa decked in J.C. Penny casuals. This wasn't initially why I had come to New Orleans.

I had sub-leased an attic room for three months on Burgundy St. in the French Quarter that boasted its own balcony space fully-equipped with wooden rocking chair. For what I was paying I could have found a place whose carpet didn't sink into moldy wood or kitchen include a toilet next to the stove. When I first told Tony what I paid monthly, he exhaled like the sip of beer on his tongue had suddenly frozen. "For two hundred square feet," he kept repeating until it was no longer a question. I shrugged while sitting on the far corner of my bed and forced a smile as if to say what-do-you-do. The embarrassment of someone knowing I badly overpaid knotted my stomach worse than the realization that I was badly overpaying, and I never mentioned the cost of my rent to anyone else.

I was to learn after my first week in New Orleans that no matter how many times I cleaned the wooden rocking chair, shiny poisonous spiders would cover it in webs, and that the balcony had a precarious tendency to lean toward the street below whenever I stood on it. However, I was an ascetic and my meager quarters suited me fine. I believed my limited comfort would push me to focus that much more on my writing.

For the first month, my living space hardly proved fruitful. I found that regardless of the hour of day, after twenty minutes of sitting in front of my small manual typewriter, I would feel the compulsion to immediately flee my surroundings. And in New Orleans it was easy to be out, because, no matter the hour, there was always something going on. For instance, these graphic designers from Iowa. As entertaining as the city was to her visitors, the visitors were entertaining to her natives, and Tony never seemed to tire of conversing with absolute strangers.

Inevitably Tony would regale these tourists with his Noah-like tales of Katrina. Most of these involved him floating pets and the elderly down streets flooded in rat- and corpse-infested waters. He had constructed makeshift rafts using hundred year-old wooden doors stripped from landmark hotels and restaurants. You could hear the screams of people still trapped in their attics needing an axe to hack their way to freedom. His Katrina stories were always punctuated with his desperate, albeit failed attempt to save his pregnant girlfriend from their first floor apartment. Tony trailed off his sentences and glazed his eyes with just enough tear-gloss to break any woman's heart.

On a slow night during my second week of frequenting the Copper Plate, Tony confided in me that he had actually been visiting extended family in Detroit during the hurricane and subsequent flooding. When he was able to return home, he realized that aside from a moldy stench permeating the clothes in his closet, he hadn't actually lost anything except a current address. If Tony's stories seemed insensitive, it could be argued that they were only insensitive in proportion to the vampiric interest most tourists showed in the New Orleans locals. Everyone wanted to know what it had been like to survive the flood. They wanted to email friends disaster tales from the ninth ward, or revel in the sensory details of the tragedy. More than once, I listened to families from places like Kensington or Lincoln interview a restaurant waitress about her experiences.

After another bar rush (another convention's arrival), Tony turned to me and asked if we should try and catch up to the Deon party. Charlie, rattling a cocktail shaker, winked at me as if to say, "You'd be crazy not to."

"Whatever," I said. "Let's leave. This spinning madness is beginning to dizzy me anyways." I had a predilection to speak in abstractions when I was buzzing from alcohol. Tony shrugged.

We closed our tabs, and Charlie made us promise to say hi for him. We made our way up to Bourbon St. to push through the drunken masses lulling in the center of the street or lured to dark doorways by baiting sironesque strippers. The whole exchange was one of my favorite things to watch and many nights I walked up and down Bourbon St. doing little more than adding mileage to my Payless Shoes. Occasionally, I wished I had the money to enter the dark establishments that boasted Live Sex shows and beautiful women (and a few times I almost convinced myself that I did have the money). I would unfold my wallet, exhale the poor man's sigh, and continue pushing dust down the street.

Tony knew some of the girls that worked at the different clubs and sometimes they visited him at The Copper Plate. While part of me was excited to listen to their stories, another part of me was disappointed by how mundane the girls appeared when not working. I'm not sure what I expected.

At the corner of Bourbon and Toulouse, I pulled Tony aside so that I could stop at a Lucky Dog cart.

"They *re-use* the water those things are cooked in. Do you get how gross that is?" He said this with so much exasperation that I felt bad disgusting him.

"Eh," I said and shrugged. I paid the stout black man and did have to admit that my whole dining experience would have been nicer if the vendor was either fully bearded or cleanly shaven. He offered me a brown-toothed smile. A moment after taking my hot dog I was distracted from the vendor by the sound of someone throwing up in the gutter just off of Bourbon.

We continued down the street passing musical bar after bar. For a city so steeped in jazz history most of the music coming from these bars was from Top 40's cover bands. It annoyed me, but the old people ate this up. They loved coming to these places and singing along to Crosby, Stills, and Nash covers or Michael Jackson's hits. My first night in New Orleans I walked into one of the these bars and was thrilled that so many people were drinking and dancing on a Wednesday night. Then I paid seven dollars for a single bottle of Bud Light.

As we walked, Tony continued to tell me stories about the different places in the Quarter that we passed. He had grown up in New Orleans and was enthusiastic about the

Quarter in a way that I didn't find common among most New Orleans natives. For Tony it was something different. It was as if he was able to see the Quarter at all points of history at once. He would tell me which doorways had been frequented by pirates, which houses used to be safe for runaway slaves. He would tell me about how Catholicism affected the businesses when the Spanish owned the city. Then he would point to a courtyard I could hardly see through the opening in the wooden gate, and he would tell me that was where he paid for his first blow job. Tony felt that he was a part of the Quarter's living history, that he was another stitch in the tapestry. I think this might have been why he was so excited to have a writer around.

I guaranteed Tony that Deon's party would be at the Paradise Disco, a flashy, techno haunt equipped with misters and lasers, but Tony wanted to start at Café Lafitte's in Exile, because he knew all of the bartenders. Once inside Tony introduced me to Howard, a bartender he used to work with at Lafitte's Blacksmith Shop, and they started talking about the highs and lows of the season. How they expected more business during the Jazz Festival.

It was then that I noticed Enrique sitting down at one of the ends of the triangular bar, half-slumped over a rocks glass. His eyes were closed, but he maintained his upright sitting position on the barstool. I walked over to him and patted him on his back careful to avoid touching his banana-thick dreadlocks. Enrique opened his eyes and turned to me with a smile (technically smiling before he even recognized who had approached him). His eyes were heavy with alcohol, and I wasn't sure he knew who I was when he said, "What up, Buddy?" I had met Enrique when hanging out on Decatur St., one of the local vegan hipsters roughly around my age. Enrique was a street musician who played his violin every afternoon either on Bourbon or Royal. He had the nappiest dreads I had ever seen on a white person.

"Not much, Enrique. Trying to find a roving birthday party. What are you up to?"

"Hustlin' . . . always hustlin'." He smiled stupidly at me, and considering our setting I was a little confused as to what "hustlin'" actually entailed.

I decided not to inquire.

"Where's Lacy?" I asked. Typically, I would find Enrique at one of the coffee shops where, when he wasn't playing his violin, he would post like a hipster pressboard collecting and distributing bits of gossip or information. There would always be a few pierced and tattooed friends sitting with him, but the only person I ever talked to other than him was a scruffy companion named Lacy who also wore her hair in long, thick dreadlocks. I had assumed they were a couple and envisioned a preternatural mating ritual involving the thick serpentine tubes of their hair dancing like cobras and intertwining like their skulls were joining squids. Now I was trying to decide whether I thought Enrique was gay.

"Write any good stories?" he asked me.

"Nothing I would call good," I said.

He thought of something and brushed two thick tendrils from his face. "This is something," he said and stood up from his barstool. He steadied himself, and, comfortable on his feet, made his way over to a table where a lone man sat sipping a drink through two cocktail straws. Replete in a seersucker suit with a firmly pressed white shirt, light colored riding shoes, and a thin diagonally striped tie, the older man sat with his legs crossed above the knee. He had almost plastically smooth skin and bright green eyes. His hair was completely white, and I couldn't tell if it had greyed to that shade or if he dyed it that color.

"Don, show my friend the paw. Show it to him," Enrique said to the man. The way Enrique was drunkenly pestering the man made me think of a gorilla trying to annoy a flamingo.

The man turned to me slowly with a placid smile and held out his hand almost as if I should kiss it. "I am Donald, and you are?"

"Gabe," I said and shook his hand weakly. It felt like dried leaves.

"Yeah, this is Gabe," said Enrique gesturing between us. "Gabe, Don. Gabe is a writer. You should show him your paw."

Donald smiled softly at Enrique and said, "I'm sorry. I don't have it with me. If you want, we can walk over to my place, and I can show it to you."

"That's ok. I can see it another time. Everyone...." I had gestured around the bar, and I think I wanted to say something about how everyone in the Quarter runs into everyone else almost daily, but the sentence died in my throat.

"I'm less than half a block away on Dumaine," Donald said. "It's really no trouble."

"Perfect," said Enrique with a hand clap. "Let's go."

"Wait, what is it I'm supposed to see? I'm sure I can check it out some other time," I said.

"No time like the present," said Donald and chuckled to himself.

"You have to see this," said Enrique. "You want to write about New Orleans? This is it."

Back at the bar Tony and Howard were talking about a woman that Howard had been seeing, two professional conversationalists hardly flexing their talents. I sensed that the conversation was less about Howard and the woman and more about Tony finding out how Howard had been, what he had been doing. For the bartenders I met, conversation was an oblique way of communicating. If you really wanted to find out what one of them thought or was up to, you had to ask about something entirely mundane. Indirect conversation was an economic advantage that these bartenders learned instinctually. The slower the conversation was they had with a patron, the more time the patron spent in the bar drinking and tipping. Direct conversation risked sending patrons stumbling down the street sooner than needed.

When I told Tony that Enrique and I were running over to Donald's place to see something, Tony groaned. "That guy is weird," Tony said scowling over his shoulder in their direction.

Howard laughed and then said, "Eccentric more than weird." Howard chopped up the syllables of the word eccentric as he said it. Their familiarity with Donald simultaneously comforted and disconcerted me. I felt reassured that I wasn't about to be murdered; though being propositioned still felt like it was on the table.

Enrique and Donald waited for me just outside the front door, and when I stepped out, Enrique stood in the street kicking the curb. The walk was short; Donald lived within throwing distance of Lafitte's. He stopped in front of a door that was painted lollipop blue. When he let us in, we found ourselves in an appallingly campy courtyard that glowed red from a single bulb burning above the space. I felt like I had entered a party store's bordello. A pink flamingo had been stuck in the dirt to my side and there was a plastic surfer floating in the Victorian fountain directly in the center of the courtyard. In the dim light, it took me a minute to recognize that the figure occupying one of the canvas lawn chairs was actually a male mannequin drenched in Mardi Gras beads and dressed in a glittery cocktail dress and a feathered headband. A few toy cars were posed on the lip of the fountain and the ground was littered with many more objects that were difficult to distinguish in the dark.

"You will have to forgive me," said Donald. "I am a bit of a collector. Please, this way."

Donald weaved his way through the tea trays and mini Santa Clauses and various-sized Trolls with the grace of someone who repeats the same combination of steps daily. Enrique plowed directly to the home's entrance, tipping over little statues and overturning a metallic fire truck. The raucous made my throat jump, but Donald waited for us in the doorway without blinking. I followed Enrique.

The front room of the house was packed with more of the same: antique lunch boxes, a phonograph, metallic poster advertisements, and long extinct logo figurines. Donald went over to a fifty year-old refrigerator and removed a bottle of gin. He waved it at us. Enrique smiled and took a seat on an old yellow couch. I declined and sat next to Enrique. When Donald brought the drinks over, Enrique was trying to open an old metallic toy car. A slight raise of Donald's eyebrow was the only sign of disapproval.

"What do you think?" Donald said to me.

I had been in houses filled with kitsch knickknacks before, but not wanting to disappoint my host I said, "I've never seen anything like this."

Donald smiled into his drink and then lightly shook the glass as if he were savoring its smell.

Enrique took a gulp from his drink and said, "Donald

has more classic stuff than anyone else in New Orleans. He's made a point to try and save things from the flood."

Donald smiled at Enrique like a proud father. "Enrique flatters me."

"Blah," said Enrique flapping his head. "Donald deals all of this stuff to restaurants and businesses all throughout the Quarter. He's rejected rich collectors from all over the world."

Donald shrugged, "I could never part with anything that was going to leave the city. These treasures belong to our home. I just want to make sure they stay here."

The notion appealed to me even though I slightly questioned Donald's altruism. There was something behind his smile that he wasn't sharing. He was too quick to show his teeth when he smiled.

Enrique broke the spell that Donald's objects cast over me and said, "Show him *it*. Come on."

Donald's mouth went wide, clearly enjoying the building suspense that Enrique added. He began, "Every great collection, it doesn't matter where in the world you go . . . every great collection has a gem. Has at least one item that crowns the rest of the collection, a keystone if you will, that without which the entire collection might collapse. Mine is no different, and several months ago, I came across something extraordinary. A young boy was referred to me, trading a family heirloom for money to save his family. I paid him well for this item . . . some might say I shorted him, but that really is a matter of opinion and while this item may be of incalculable value to me, it is only because I have spent a lifetime making the connections that I made. If anything Katrina offered me the greatest windfall of all—two great changes in this city occurred. For one, everything that I possessed became extremely valuable as the sea stole comparable pieces from others. And, two, suddenly people needed money to start their lives over and were willing to part with objects that did little more than collect mold in their closets."

"And all of the kids pillaging old houses," said Enrique with a laugh.

Donald frowned, "I never paid for anything that didn't come directly to me through its owner." His argument seemed dubious and unverifiable. Enrique shook his head to himself and chuckled.

Donald exhaled audibly and then reached over to a polished chestnut case to his side. He took a small key from his pocket and popped it into the case. With a twist the case was open, but all I could see was the green felt padding. When he handed it to me, I stared dumbly at the contents.

"I suppose you wonder why I don't keep something like this locked in a safety deposit box," Donald continued. "Why I don't even own a safe. The reason is simple. All of my pieces are entirely valueless without the right connections. I have nothing to fear, because I have found a way to store all of my value in my mind. Without the things I know, all of this," he gestured around the room, "is worth nothing."

I was staring at a shrunken black claw-like hand. I had no idea what it was, but it appeared delicate and I was hesitant to touch it. I looked at Enrique trying to figure out if I was participating in some elaborate prank, and then looked at Donald who stared at me with a steady, solemn expression. I started to say something, but stopped.

"You don't know what that is, do you?" said Donald. This made his brow relax. "In this room is the single largest private collection of pieces from New Orleans' history. I have amassed everything I could from the jazz and Dixie era, and even souvenirs from the Spanish and French colonial periods before that. But what you hold in your hands is the one thing that transcends all of those periods. It is something that comes from the original natives of this land. It is a lupin claw, that is, a werewolf's hand probably from the sixteenth century. The last remnant of an extinct people that used to inhabit this delta."

The little paw appeared delicately skeletal with a paper-thin, dried vellum stretched over it. It was small, maybe the size of a child's hand with rounded black nails that pointed like a dog's. The skin had retracted at the cuticles.

I lifted the box up and down a few times but couldn't gauge the weight of the claw from the weight of its expensive wooden case.

"That's it, right?" Enrique asked. "That's what you've been looking for?" He laughed a touch maniacally.

"This is the birth of New Orleans," Donald said and spread his arms open to encompass his surroundings.

I had nothing to say. I had traveled to find something unique in New Orleans and had embraced a culture that I thought was specific to the Quarter, but up until the moment of staring at the claw, I hadn't realized that there was something intrinsic to these people that would always prohibit me from truly understanding them. Something in that strange claw eluded me...and whatever it was that I couldn't grasp...the thing that was capable of transfixing both Enrique and Donald...and all of the other locals who spoke about it in the few days following...it was that thing that struck me mute. This inexplicable essence erected walls between me and the city, those people. There was nothing I could do to reach them.

Within a week my bags were packed and I had moved

on. I caught a bus heading away from the river and settled in New York where different things were asked of me. But these were things I could give. It took me a long time to learn how to write a sentence again.

KEEP SHUFFLING STEPS

I spend the afternoon sketching people in Alphabet City. I love capturing the way the skaters sit around the edges of Tompkins Square Park. They remind me of Tony and all of his friends. Their postures curve like lowercase S's when they sit on their boards, laughing and getting high, punching each other. Later I will come back to mix my palette for the right hues to capture their style and grime, the bright t-shirts and punk rock flairs dampened with dirt, body oil, and grease. Raw sienna and yellow ochre for their denim fray.

My little brother was a skate rat and used to spend most of his time palling around with a pack of skaters at the mall parking lot near our apartment....

Dominic comes over and offers a pull from his paper-bagged forty. He tells me he's trying to get some friends together to run a roving renegade craft table. Try to sell some cheap handcrafts to the tourists in between police patrols. Do I want in? I could make a bill a day he figures. Tourists have money.

"Sounds like I'll have to yell at a lot of strangers," I say.

"Pshhaw. Gypsies lay down a blanket with their handmade, garbage-bead jewelry and sell by the bagfuls.

They don't have to say shit," he says. He shakes his head, throws a crooked-tooth smile at me and extends his hand as if to say you-know-me. He takes another pull from his bottle.

"What's it to you? I don't get what you have to do with any of this." In the City, everyone takes. There are no charities without fingers in the pocket. You have to train yourself to look for the angles.

"Simple economics, *amico*. I suck at art. I have all of these ideas." Dominic snaps his fingers agitatedly to emphasize the sparks of his thoughts. "I know so many artists who spin their wheels, but catch no friction. They either turn their art into a hobby or they eventually quit altogether. They cross the bridge. Become suburban." He sneers and taps my upper arm with his hand. "This project is a collective of artists that I personally invite. I am creating a mobile art gallery called D Space. Everyone takes turns running the D Space for a day. I start advertising online on all of the art web pages; I tap into the tourism pages; I get a buzz going in the Voice. The hook is that D Space will have no fixed location. It will appear all over the island for a day at a time, and people will have to go to the website or have a friend that spots it. My cousin told me about a food cart in Portland that works like this. That city is full of food carts, but people scour the city trying to buy food from this one cart. It is a ghost. It has cache."

"But if your artists are selling their art...what do you get?"

"No tricks. You sell your art in a gallery, they charge you fifty percent. This is an industry standard. You sell your stuff for a day through D Space. I get twenty percent. It's your pennies for dollars. I create a market for you, I take just a little."

It isn't unreasonable assuming Dominic does the PR legwork. He was known as a small-time promoter and hustler, but the fact is that some things *did* happen under his guidance. The hipsters were wearing the Chuck Norris shirts he printed. Dominic got Richie to busk for a Summer near the ferry port. It didn't last long, but Richie made a lot of green while doing it.

I tell him I am in. We slide a handshake into a fist bump to seal the deal.

I head back to the apartment buzzing, thoughts of new projects and sell strategies swimming through my mind. I am thinking of small, readily producible sketches on poster board. I can hustle five dollar frames from the pharmacy. The sun fades down Houston Street as the City transitions to night. The hipsters flip hanging Open signs to Closed in the boutiques; the pubs and restaurants begin to fill. I look through the windows at the people taking advantage of Happy Hour. Sweaty glasses of cold beer and plates of Buffalo wings or pitas sit neglected in front of smiling, chatty faces and healthy bodies layered in clean, expensive clothes. I have to believe that they are all trust-fund brats; it would break my heart to hear about someone my age making significant money.

I have sixty-eight cents in my pocket, all scavenged from the couch cushions this morning. I have been fingering the two quarters, dime, nickel and pennies in my pocket for hours daydreaming about the Watermelon Jolly Rancher I will buy. These thoughts became all the more pronounced after I ran out of water.

At TJ's Market on the corner of my block, Rasheed doesn't hassle me about refilling my trucker's mug with water. He rings me up for the Jolly Rancher asking me about my day, and we trade plans for the night with elaborate explanations about why we won't be going to the bars we won't be going to. I ask after his new son. When little Prabaker was born I gave Rasheed a drawing of a waving teddy bear as a gift to decorate the baby's room.

We joke about the tyranny of daily occupation, and I thank Rasheed for the water. I push out the swinging door of the market with the dangling jingle bells tied to the door handle punctuating my exit.

I consider sitting on the planter stoop next door and tearing into my candy, but decide to continue back to the apartment instead on the hunch that Colleen may be eating her dinner right now.

No flower in the window.

Our building has two distinctions that welcome me home. The first distinction is the temperamental front door, which will often leave one shaking it to no avail after having entered the keypad code successfully. The second distinction is a particular musty scent unlike any other building I have entered in the City. This scent is comprised of the common mold-plus-rust scent, but infused with a slightly sour cheese. It is a particular stink that has come to make me feel at home the moment it hits my nostrils.

When I enter the apartment Colleen waves to me from the kitchen while stirring what appears to be soup and talking into the cell phone that is nestled between her ear and shoulder. She appears only half put together, her hair coiffed and face made-up, but wearing sweatpants and a t-shirt. I unshoulder my bag and swing it to the foot of the couch on which I sleep. I collapse onto my ruffled pillow and blanket. Unzipping my shoulder bag, I dig through the day's sketches and transfer them to the large portfolio I keep between the couch and the end table. This folder, a backpack full of clothing, and a small case of art supplies amount to my only possessions. My Spartan existence is a necessity.

Colleen hangs up the phone and comes into the front with a steaming bowl of soup in her hands. I watch her hips swing as she walks, her midriff exposed between the low-riding sweatpants and tight t-shirt.

"That was another asshole from the agency trying to blow me off," she says. Colleen is trying to get modeling work.

"You wouldn't happen to have a spare bowl, would you?" I raise my eyebrows to appear more charming. She pauses and looks at me with annoyance. I don't blink.

"Go for it," she nods her head toward the kitchen.

As I ladle myself a bowl she says, "Save me my bread. That's the last of it." I see the bread and tell her I will, but when she isn't looking I tear off a corner of it and submerge it into my soup. Now I can save my Jolly Rancher for later.

Walking back in the front room she tells me, "You really need to start picking up some extra shifts." She stares at her soup as she says this. Her eyelashes flap like butterfly wings when she blinks. She is a hard taskmadam. I have three shifts a week bussing tables at a restaurant.

"I told the manager already. He's got me on call. I'm totally going to do that," I say. "In the meantime, Dominic invited me to join an art collective he is creating. He wants to sell some of my art."

"That fake dago douche is such a tool."

"Maybe, but if I can get paid, I don't care." We slurp our soup for a minute, and I worry she may try and turn on the TV so I ask, "What've you been up to today?"

"I woke up and researched some fashion trends and then tried to network on some modeling blogs. Then I circled a few boutiques and made some calls." I love the way she describes dicking around on the internet and shopping. Colleen is so ridiculous, and I love her for it. I decide in that moment to make out with her this evening. In my head I start formulating a plan that involves shoplifting some liquor and blasting some 80's rock out of her little stereo. Trying to create a party atmosphere at home. Out loud I tell her about the sketches I made today. As soon as we finish our soup, I will show her.

There is a knock on the door. It sounds like my dreams being punched in the stomach, but it feels like castration. I think through a silent prayer. Colleen's eyes are the size of silver dollars as she tiptoes to the door. She peers through the peephole and then casts me a look that I will forever attempt to sketch. One day I will paint her image with this look: in front of a door, head turned looking over her shoulder, mouth sealed but eyes telling the whole story.

I stand up, tuck my pillow and blanket under my arm, throw my backpack and shoulder bag over my other shoulder, grab the soup bowl in one hand and my portfolio folder in the other. In the kitchen I quietly set the soup bowl and spoon into the sink and then round the corner to the bedroom. I hear Colleen open the door and Mike's heavy footsteps enter the apartment. I can hear them talking as I silently slip the portfolio into the back of Colleen's closet. I throw my blanket and pillow on her messy bed. She turns on the television to give me a little white noise as I make my escape.

Before I go, I peak through the slightly cracked door and see Mike putting his hands all over Colleen. He says, "No, you look so much hotter to me this way." He smashes his face into hers with so much aggression I can practically see his tongue flailing around in her mouth through her cheeks. I turn to the window, slide it up slowly, slip onto the fire escape. I descend a floor before I pause for a minute to fasten my backpack properly onto my back and readjust my shoulder bag.

I used to be nervous stepping onto a fire escape four floors up. I used to have to hold the iron railing with one hand the whole way down. All of my possessions are on my back like I'm a snail. Now I hope that the escape collapses and crushes me. A useless snail.

I think about my friends from Jersey starting art school this past month. They spend their mornings studying art and their afternoons painting in giant studios. I want to call them at this moment. I want to check in with them and hear about their lives for a little while. I want to make up lies about my own life.

We graduated high school knowing two things about becoming an artist: sacrifice yourself for a woman that will never love you and surrender yourself to the crushing cogs of the City. These were the spices to throw in the sauté: the artist's gestation, a sprinkle of heartbreak over the metropolitan bildungsroman. We fantasized about living six deep in one-room studios in the East Village and subsidizing our diets with discount cat food tins while we painted portraits of our respective muses in blood, food grease, and tears. We mentally prepared for the all-night benders that would begin halfway through our working nights, our livers thoroughly soaked in gin and vodka, when we would be interrupted by tearful phone calls that sent us running down rainy blocks and culminated in third-story-window-to-sidewalk screaming matches with our spurned lovers only to return to our rooms defeated and produce such bristling, incendiary works of art, works that shore so much of our zeitgeist that by the time art dealers discovered us and threw millions at us, hosted three-star catered gallery openings in our honor; it no longer mattered to us, the fame, the fortune, whisked lightly off the crushed husks of our souls, like a draft taking the ashes of our love letters we had already incinerated in an empty coffee can on the floor of our room.

This was how we thought about art.

I had been in love with Colleen since ninth grade when she stayed a few minutes after the seventh period bell to compliment one of the huge drawings I was working on of a factory warehouse. She stayed to tell me how much she liked the pictures I drew, to discuss our favorite pencils (seemed arbitrary and stupid, but I told her 2B), and to talk about how even though Van Gogh daubed the vibrant colors, Goya was the true master contending with everything from social injustice to artistic insanity. The whole time we spoke she kept rolling her eyes and brushing her bangs to the side and speaking with clipped words as if she were the one who was nervous in my presence.

I don't think we really said that stuff about the artists, but I remember every detail of her smile/eye-roll/hair-brush. That night I made the first sketch of her, one that I would re-sketch, draw, and eventually make her sit for me as I painted with fine bristle brushes. These were our high school years when we spent hours together roaming the city, sneaking into free movies, hanging out at the corner table of the McDonald's, and spending too much money for photos at school dances. The two of us a couple of chuckling clowns sticking our tongues out and crossing our eyes in the Package A eight-by-tens.

These photos were lost in the apartment fire, which adds significance to the memory of them. It is more pleasant to remember the small stack of photos rather than the frustrating times when the world felt like a series of injustices. If it weren't for the bathroom mirror I would forget to notice the star I carved into my shoulder with the piece of the beer bottle she'd thrown at me after we fought in the church parking lot across the street from Adam's party. I had tried to kiss her, which was against her rules, and I was passionate in my rejection.

There were the tearful phone calls we dragged out for hours while I explained categorically why we had to be in love, and she listened with patience and said, yes, but not that kind of love. Secretly, I knew these conversations were telegraphing the impossibility of our relationship, but I would struggle against the tide only taking solace in having fought the heroic fight.

We didn't talk to each other much of our senior year of high school. I would eye her coolly across the hall, but she wouldn't even cast me a glance. In the fall I applied to three art schools. Near Christmas of that year, my family's apartment building caught fire. It happened in the afternoon when both my parents were at work. I was at school, but my little brother Tony had skipped class and was asleep on the couch. Certain walls of our apartment and most of our possessions were consumed, but Tony had succumbed to asphyxiation, as if the fire had attempted to steal his voice. I thought about the conversations we will never have. The weeks around Christmas were a blur of impermanent settings and a hasty funeral where many of Tony's classmates showed up. I don't remember much about it.

The next thing I remember vividly is the first day back at school and having to look up from green marble tile of the hallways to catch everyone right in the pupils. A few months later I received the acceptance letters to the art schools and frantically tried to salvage the possibility that

I could go. When I tried to bring up art school with my father he dismissed me saying, blood from a stone. My mother wouldn't even take her eyes from the television. She had stopped talking to me after Tony died. A part of me knew it was a hopeless fight; my parents' lives were now in shambles. But I also don't think my father the carpenter or my mother the R.N. would have understood my art school ambitions even without the fire.

By spring I had begun to settle into the mediocrity of my life. I had grown sour in the realization that I would definitely not be in school the next year. My father had arranged for me to start routing cabinets at a mill the week after I graduated, and he was immovable when I pleaded for him to allow me to at least go on a senior trip with my friends. His logic was severe: finish school, pay rent. As I had no money, I had no leverage to argue and conceded to his demands in the end.

The high school graduation ceremony was forgettable. To punctuate our achievement, the more wicked of us threw our caps sideways like spiraling Chinese stars hoping that one of the cardboard corners would catch a recipient in the face. At a graduation house party, I got drunk on champagne and tried to make out with the high school slut. I started crying before we kissed.

The Santinelli Mill was run by a sadistic humored man who took pleasure in watching me learn about woodworking the hard way. When the router jerked one of my cabinet doors and dislocated my finger, Sam ran around the mill clutching my wrist and dragging me in his wake to show everyone "my funny finger." During my first couple of days, I was feeding the industrial planer when the hum changed to a whine and the blade caught the board and threw it back into my testicles. As I rolled on the floor worrying about whether I had lost any body parts, Sam raced over out of breath with laughter to tell me that the moment he heard the machine's whine change he grabbed Rick and Jason, because they all knew what was going to happen.

Three days out of high school and I was locked into a sixty-hour work week schedule with a handful of lifers who shuffled through each day until they could go home to drink a few beers and a yell at a baseball game.

At the beginning of August I received a phone call.

"Hey." I may have been overly sentimental, but Colleen's voice sounded like drippy disco fries.

"How's it going?"

"Guess where I'm standing," she said. I could hear traffic in the background.

"In the middle of the Red Sea?"

"Two blocks from the Empire State Building. I'm watching the sunlight work its way up the building as the sun sets."

I didn't have anything to say to that, so I waited.

"I didn't know if you still had the same phone number—"

"Yep." The fire. Really, we have to talk about the fire now, too. A conversation, half a year too late.

She changed tactics. "How's your Summer going?" she asked.

"Fan-tast-ic. My dad worked it out so that I work in this mill all day. I can actually hear my soul choking on the sawdust that fills my lungs. It's great...what are you doing?"

"Living in the City. I went to New York on senior trip and met this guy, who had a place I could stay in the City. He is trying to help me start my modeling career. Everyday I go to auditions and try to network with designers. I don't have to pay rent and the guy will give me food money. It's a shithole, but I can't complain."

"You trying to marry this guy or something?"

"No…it's not like that. He's just a friend. Has a family already. He's on Wall Street and is just helping me out."

"Sounds…good." It always knocks the knees out from me when I hear someone confidently state a really bad idea. I can remember in eighth grade when Dustin explained that he was only going to smoke weed once an evening, or listening to my father explain to my mother an investment opportunity one of his buddies at the refinery was lauding.

"You know, I have the space…you could crash on the couch. You give me two hundred bucks a month. Cheapest rent on the island."

Fear and excitement ran up and down me simultaneously. I knew this was an important chance, but I was still a little afraid to leave the nest. "What about your guy? What will he think?"

"That is the tricky part. I don't think he would like me subletting this place. But we could work out a system."

The way she described it to me sounded like a noble artistic adventure. I could only take a few possessions. I would keep my stuff in a bag. She would put a flower in the window on the outside of the curtains if I needed to stay away. I would be in the City, I would be making art, and I would be living in an illegal squat.

My romance with my situation was crushed the first night I spent on the street. Colleen hadn't entirely explained her relationship with Mike to me. During one of his first impromptu visits, I was too scared to climb out the fire escape, so I hid in the closet. For an hour I listened to them fucking. As a virgin, I couldn't comprehend casual sex. I kept thinking that there had to be a victim.

I felt my chest rip to pieces, and I thought of stepping out of the closet and killing Mike. Killing Colleen, too. Killing the whole world. Anything to stop the pain. I tried to think of myself as a hero, that my suffering was valiant. That pain was the only true teacher of passion. I was learning. I was being made.

Colleen had just closed the front door behind Mike when I stepped out of the bedroom. She had no idea I was there. We stood there for a minute in silence.

"I hid in the closet. You are a prostitute."

She charged me and pushed my chest. "Fuck you," she screamed. She tried to claw my face and gradually drove me toward the front door and told me to get the fuck out of her home. I was crying, but that only made her madder. She slammed the door on me.

I spent a long night walking the city. The air was warm, which was a relief, because I didn't have a blanket or a sleeping bag and was almost entirely unprepared to sleep without shelter. I just spent the night drifting from one location to the next. I tried to milk any stop I made as long as I could and conserve my energy. My backpack and shoulder bag began to get heavy, and I tried to think of places I could stash them for the night, maybe a series of bushes that would stay untouched or in one of those lockers that drug dealers in movies always use. Where are those? Train stations, airports? I don't think airports even have those anymore. Where is the closest train station?

I rode the subway for an hour, but it made me sleepy and that made me nervous. I kept angrily eyeing any other aimless passengers. I changed trains every fifteen minutes for fear of riding too far out of my familiarity zone. I hadn't been in New York long, had only ridden the subway a few times and was still unsure of how the trains ran at night. I was petrified of being marooned in a dangerous neighborhood. I still wasn't even sure where the dangerous neighborhoods were.

At midnight I had been absolutely determined never to see Colleen again. I devised plans to stay in the city and make it without ever seeing her again. At least not until I was famous and she sheepishly reintroduced herself to me at one of my plush gallery openings. Spending a night stranded in New York seemed easy. I had stayed up all night tons of times.

By three in the morning, all I wanted more than anything else in life was to be able to go back to the apartment and fall asleep on the couch. What kept gnawing at me was the notion that I couldn't go back if I wanted. It was easy to stay up all night with the comfort that there was a bed waiting for you, but it was far more difficult when that bed didn't exist.

The same imaginary scenarios circled my thoughts like drooling vultures. I could wait outside the apartment building and cry and plead with her to take me back. I would beg for a place to sleep and shower. I was so tired I think I was enacting these fantasies out loud and really crying. Strangers avoided me.

I gave up hope of surviving the night; my exhaustion was so severe I began losing touch with reality. The whole world had become surreal. At one point I had an extended conversation with a cloaked figure about the possibility that angels in the past were disguised as unicorns. I wanted Tony to be underneath that hood. I was excited to share with him my theories about dragons. Why did they exist in both eastern and western mythological traditions? I tried to remember what he looked like, my little brother's vivid face talking to me, but I couldn't put it together. My impressions of memories would fall away if I tried to analyze them.

Gradually, I became aware that the intensity of the streetlights was waning. The space between buildings was beginning to take a soft gray hue. I had made it to dawn. This reinvigorated me and without a second thought, I began making my way back to the apartment. I don't know why, but I had decided that my trial was over.

The sun had almost crested by the time I walked into our building. My feet felt heavy plodding up the stairs, and I thought of the fur-wrapped feet of Vikings returning to their homeland. A part of me hoped for an Odyssey-style homecoming: a huge celebratory feast culminating in a bloodbath.

My courage dropped like curtains at the doorway, and I knocked with a mousey tap. On my second series of knocks the door opened, and Colleen and I looked at each other. We both looked worn. She opened the door for me and then went off to bed without a word. I had hoped for an emotional reconciliation, but was tired as well.

By the disarray of blanket and pillow on the couch I could tell that she had slept there waiting for me. I lay in her smell all day fantasizing about her concern and worry. It was one of my most beautiful days of sleep.

It is the kind of sleep that keeps me shuffling my steps now.

ABOUT THE AUTHOR

Christopher Steffen spent a formative number of years living in Salt Lake City. He fled to the Bay Area to live in a tiny apartment in Oakland and work menial jobs in the serving industry. When not maintaining the split blog Path to Literary Success/Path to Literary Failure, he can be found furiously scribbling into a yellowed journal. He may be making your coffee drink, bringing you your entrée, or mixing you a cocktail. He may deliver your suitcases to your room. Tip generously. Thank you.